The
Counterfeit
COWGIRL

KATHRYN BROCATO

Author of *Old Christmas, Sutherland's Pride,*
and *Georgio's Heart*

CRIMSON
ROMANCE

F+W Media, Inc.

This edition published by
Crimson Romance
an imprint of F+W Media, Inc.
10151 Carver Road, Suite 200
Blue Ash, Ohio 45242
www.crimsonromance.com

ISBN 10: 1-4405-7245-3
ISBN 13: 978-1-4405-7245-6
eISBN 10: 1-4405-7244-5
eISBN 13: 978-1-4405-7244-9

This Book is Dedicated to
My Mother
Margery Fay Coffman King
Who always wanted to be a Cowgirl

Chapter 1

"Hey, babe, is the rodeo in town?"

The admiring words came from a tall, rangy man in a cowboy hat who lounged against a car parked outside the grocery store. Felicity Clayton tossed an impersonal smile at him. She had been worried that people in Foxe, the small Southeast Texas Gulf Coast town where she'd just arrived, wouldn't take notice of her clothes.

So much for that fear. She'd attracted plenty of notice while shopping in the grocery store and was still attracting attention in the parking lot.

From the slim blue denim skirt that skimmed the tops of her high-heeled cowboy boots to the red bandanna-print shirt, Felicity might have just ridden in off the high-fashion range. Even her hair fit the look. She had pulled the shoulder-length brown mass off her face in deference to the Gulf Coast heat and humidity and fastened it at the nape of her neck with a leather clasp that matched her boots.

A turquoise and silver necklace and ring matched the handcrafted silver belt at her waist, and silver horses dangled from her ears. She completed her eye-catching outfit with a leather purse that resembled a miniature saddle. Her purse held a sheaf of business cards bearing the logo of The Cosmic Cowgirl, the western boutique Felicity owned in Nashville, Tennessee.

"You look...mmm, mmm good, babe," the man added. "A little skinny for my taste, but you sure got class."

Felicity winked at the rumpled pseudo-cowboy. As a slim woman with nondescript brown hair and brown eyes, she figured she needed all the help she could get from stylish clothing. Otherwise, she might fade into brown anonymity.

"Thanks, cowboy," she said and prepared to climb into her shiny, white pickup.

"Buzz off, Leroy," a deep, gravelly voice said.

The voice carried overtones of suppressed anger that attracted Felicity's attention. Whoever it was sounded like Johnny Cash. Turning, she stared at a veritable mountain of a man who was climbing down from a dusty blue truck that had just pulled into the parking lot.

He was over six feet tall, with broad, capable shoulders and thick, dark hair. Felicity didn't blame Leroy for leaving the scene immediately. The new arrival looked madder than a wet bantam rooster.

"He wasn't bothering me, but thanks anyway." Her impersonal smile turned into a mischievous grin when she noted the effect the braces on her teeth appeared to have on him. He winced and closed navy-blue eyes.

She caught her breath. Something about him urged her to put extra energy into her smile.

"I'd like to speak to you a moment, Miss Clayton." He slammed the door of his truck aggressively.

Yes, the man was definitely angry. That and the fact that he knew her name made Felicity doubly wary.

"You have the advantage of knowing my name, Mr....?"

"Whitaker," he said in a clipped, furious tone. "Aaron Whitaker. Not that it matters. You probably won't be here any longer than it takes to get the money and run."

Felicity's brows lifted in astonishment. "I don't know what you're talking about, Mr. Whitaker. But it's a pleasure to meet you, anyway." She held out her hand.

Felicity was accustomed to a certain amount of hostility from men with fashionable wives who spent a lot of money in her shop. She was always at her friendliest when meeting them. Except that nobody here knew who she was. Perhaps she sold him a piece of farm equipment a few years back when she had traveled the South selling tractors and combines to farmers.

She studied Aaron Whitaker, refusing to let him rattle her. Saleswomen grew impervious to negative reactions, or they didn't stay in sales very long. Besides, without his height and those rugged, tanned features, his contemptuous stare wouldn't have had nearly as much impact. His mouth, a masterpiece of chiseled, stony disapproval, and his square jaw both added to the impression of tough implacability.

She made it impossible for him to ignore her proffered hand. He took it automatically and she noticed his palm was hard with calluses.

She let her gaze glide down him. Weathered, form-fitting jeans hugged his long, muscular legs. He wore scuffed cowboy boots, and a blue work shirt had been rolled up to expose muscular, tanned forearms liberally sprinkled with dark hair.

No wonder he disapproved of her. He was a genuine cowboy fresh off the range, and she was a fashion-house fake. She had never even ridden a horse—at least, not long enough to call it riding. She was all show, whereas this man was the genuine article. Well, too bad. In her line of business, image was everything.

"You favor the cowboy look, I see," she said, and smiled approvingly. "It suits you."

"It doesn't suit you. You look like a rhinestone rodeo queen." He appeared to realize he was still holding her hand and dropped it. "But that's beside the point."

"It's not beside the point if you have any interest at all in fashion." She bared her silver-banded teeth at him. "If I sold men's clothing, I'd offer you a huge salary to advertise for me. You're the perfect example of a working cowboy."

Aaron looked as though he'd just swallowed a huge dose of ipecac syrup. He half shut his eyes, as if the glare from her braces blinded him.

"It's the jeans and the boots," Felicity said helpfully.

"I don't give a damn about fashion." He regarded her with a curious combination of annoyance and dawning respect.

"I see," Felicity said.

A saleswoman had to keep her skills honed. Besides, Aaron's obvious contempt brought out Felicity's besetting sin, the urge to convert people to her point of view. "You favor the man-of-the-earth image. A pair of steel-toed boots—"

"I don't favor any such image," Aaron snapped. "Shut up for a minute, will you?"

Felicity arranged her face into a smile of bland interest. "I'm holding my breath in anticipation, cowboy."

Aaron's expression turned as bland as hers. "You won't be for long. Especially if you're the woman who now owns Lureen Tucker's house."

He threw that out like a challenge. Felicity wondered where Aaron came by his information. She did own Lureen Tucker's house and had for the past five years. Far be it from her to enlighten him, she decided, taking in his scornful navy gaze and ruggedly disapproving expression.

"My breath is still on hold." She ignored the trickle of sweat down her back and the damp feel of her heavy denim skirt. Standing in the direct glare of the sun on a humid September afternoon threatened to take the starch out of her, but she wasn't about to let Aaron Whitaker know that. "What does the ownership of a house have to do with anything?"

Aaron flashed his teeth once more. "Ordinarily, neighborliness is something I prize. In your case, however, I'm making an exception."

She had no idea what he meant, although she experienced a sinking feeling when she recollected the large brick, ranch-style house some distance from her own little wood-frame house. Glancing over his shoulder, she reaffirmed the sinking feeling. The blue pickup was the same double-cab truck parked in the wide, circular drive at the house next door to hers.

"A child could easily fall down that hole you call a well in the back yard." He pinned her with an accusing stare. "I expect that nuisance to be properly covered by tomorrow morning, or I'll sue you. Is that clear?"

"I'm sorry to hear that, Mr. Whitaker." She couldn't believe this. "If there's an open well in my backyard, I'll certainly see to covering it."

"See that you do." Aaron gave her a dangerous smile, his eyes glittering. "Mrs. Tucker says you're all business. Not one penny of profit escapes you, according to her. Now that I've seen you for myself, it's obvious where every penny goes."

Suddenly, everything became clear. Felicity sucked in her breath as annoyance replaced her puzzlement.

"I do think first appearances are so important," she purred. "Don't you, Mr. Whitaker?"

The expression on the cowboy's face was priceless.

"In that case," he said, "maybe you'll see to getting your property mowed and having that eyesore of a house painted. Otherwise, people are sure to get an impression of you I'm sure you don't want them to have."

Felicity was dumbfounded. She had arrived in Foxe barely three hours ago, and already she had made an enemy.

Usually, she never made enemies unless she outsold some of the non-producing, entrenched salespeople. Usually, even her enemies liked her. In fact, Felicity was accustomed to being liked because she always took care to make her colleagues in the sales department look good. What was wrong with Aaron?

She forced a nonchalant shrug. "Sorry, Mr. Whitaker. I haven't been in town long enough to fully assess the property and what needs to be done to it. But you can rest assured that by the time I leave here, that property will be in bandbox condition."

She could safely promise him that. Cleaning, repairing, and selling that house was the reason she was spending her first vacation in years in Foxe. Some vacation…barely one day into it, and already the house was causing trouble.

"We'll see," Aaron said, eyes narrowed with dislike. "A woman like you is usually full of promises she can't—or won't—keep."

"A woman like me?" she echoed, baffled. "What—?"

"Just tell me this." Aaron's voice dripped with contempt. "Was Lureen Tucker your grandmother?"

Felicity felt her face flush. "She was. However—"

"How many times did you visit her in the five years she lived here?"

Felicity's mouth opened, but Aaron cut her off. Worse, two other cars had pulled into the parking lot and she sensed the avid interest of the drivers.

"Well, let me tell you something, cowgirl. I have no use for a woman who treats elderly people like throwaways. That old lady might have been a little spooky, but she was still your grandmother. You never visited her once in all the years I've known her. Neither has anyone else in your so-called family. I happen to know her only visitor was an old guy named Fenton Mills."

Felicity opened her mouth again, but for once the Saleswoman of the Year for three years running failed to get a word in edgewise.

"No one in my family wants anything to do with you. Get that house into some kind of decent shape, then kindly get out of our lives and stay out."

"Do you have any knowledge at all of what you're talking about?" Felicity asked, when she recovered her power of speech.

Aaron smiled. The gesture reminded Felicity of a wolf showing its teeth. "That well is an accident waiting to happen, and now that you've been informed of it, you're going to be held responsible if anything happens before you can get it covered. You'd better pray one of my dogs doesn't fall down that thing."

He turned and bounded into his dusty pickup with a single, powerful motion. He backed out swiftly, without squealing his tires, and drove off without so much as a glance in the rear view mirror.

She stared after him. It looked as though establishing herself as a responsible businesswoman and a good neighbor during her brief stay in Foxe was going to be harder than she thought.

Well, she relished a challenge; nothing was any fun if it came too easily. Still, she was unused to being disliked, and dislike was the dominant emotion on Aaron's face when he'd told her to repair the house and stay away from his family. It was amazing how deflated she felt after the small confrontation, even though she knew the truth about Lureen Tucker and he, apparently, didn't.

"Is everything all right?" The tow-headed teen who helped load her groceries earlier, grinned at her. Country music's hottest female star, Becky Lozano, erupted from his earbuds loud enough to be clearly heard as he approached. "Old Aaron looked pretty put out."

"Who is he?" Felicity asked. "He looks like he just rode in off the cattle range."

"He does own about a hundred head of Red Brahmans," the boy said cheerfully. "But you don't make much off them." He nodded at her truck. "He owns the Chevrolet dealership a mile or so down the highway. Maybe he's mad because you're driving a Dodge."

Felicity glanced affectionately at her new white truck. A thick crust of tiny black insects covered the grill and dotted the hood and windshield. "That's probably it. Are you a Becky Lozano fan?"

"You bet I am." The teenager patted the pocket containing his MP3 player. "Every year, I pray they'll get her to sing at the Rice Festival."

"Maybe they will." She had seen the billboard signs advertising this year's Rice Festival when she drove into town. Thankfully, Becky Lozano wouldn't be anywhere near Foxe during the festival.

"The festival's in a couple of weeks, isn't it?" she asked, just to be sure.

"That's right, ma'am. They've got Randy MacElroy as headline entertainer this year."

Felicity grinned. "That should thrill the ladies."

"Yes, ma'am."

Her denim skirt and bandanna-print blouse clung damply to her skin by the time she climbed into her truck and switched on the radio. Becky Lozano's mellow, Kentucky Hills voice reached out, but before the melody could wrap itself around her, Felicity punched the off-button.

Which reminded her; she needed to buy a new cell phone. Hers appeared to have no service in Foxe. Felicity thought about going in search of one and decided against it. She would enjoy the peace and quiet for maybe one more day.

Dozens of the little black flies that covered the hood of her truck floated in the still air. She supposed she'd better get her truck washed—that was another job for tomorrow.

She turned off the highway and drove down the country road to the house, admiring the flat, green pastures and picturesque, grazing cattle. Rice fields and levees bordered with tallow trees formed a patchwork pattern that was unusual to eyes accustomed to green Tennessee hills. The peaceful scene was unexpectedly soothing.

The whole thing with Aaron Whitaker was a misunderstanding, she decided. He was bound to apologize when he discovered the facts, and when she got the problem with the well corrected— assuming there was a problem. Felicity pictured herself accepting Aaron's apology and grew more cheerful as she imagined an abashed expression on those rugged features.

She turned into the shell-covered driveway of her temporary home, bounced across a couple of ruts, and mentally noted to call out a driveway repairman, along with a lawn-care service and a water well covering business.

Glancing next door—which was far enough away to require a pair of binoculars if she wanted to observe details—Felicity scowled at the dusty blue pickup. Then she noticed an unusual air of excitement about the pristine landscape. Aaron himself stood near the neatly trimmed hedge that separated their two properties, frantically calling someone.

Felicity pointedly ignored him but continued to watch the action out of the corner of her eye. A slim young woman repeated Aaron's actions at the other end of the wide, spreading lawn. Perhaps she was Aaron's wife. A third woman, whom Felicity took to be the housekeeper, ran out of the house and toward a sprawling building at the rear of the property.

Felicity climbed out of her truck with keys in one hand, a sack of cleaning supplies balanced on her other arm, and her gaze fixed on the search. No doubt one of Aaron's dogs had gotten loose and taken off for parts unknown. Felicity experienced a twinge of sympathy for the dog, although she told herself it would serve Aaron right to lose a valuable dog—probably a bull terrier or a Rottweiler. Furthermore, he had no right to drag his poor wife out in the afternoon heat to search for his stupid dog. Felicity grew indignant over his thoughtlessness.

Thoughts of the well out back gave her a twinge of fright, but she vanquished that quickly. If she knew Aaron, and she thought she did after that one brief meeting, he had already checked out the well, probably hoping he'd find the dog at the bottom of it so he could sue her.

She held the grocery sack carefully so the rattle of the paper wouldn't interfere with her snooping and tiptoed across the creaking, wooden porch. Whoever heard of naming a dog Pete? Or Joey?

Perhaps Aaron's children had gone missing. But surely he'd have mentioned them instead of his dogs when he told her about her uncovered well. No, Pete and Joey must be Aaron's dogs.

She frowned. Perhaps the dogs were a matched set of schnauzers like the ones she saw at a friend's house last week in Nashville. Their real names were probably something like Joleibenshen's Benckenstein Venerschnitzel. They probably possessed shelves full of dog show trophies and a sheaf of pedigree papers.

Felicity decided she'd been too harsh. The dogs were probably house pets unused to the humid late summer temperatures of the Gulf Coast. She couldn't let two beautiful schnauzers, or whatever kind of dog he had lost, suffer because Aaron Whitaker was a judgmental jerk.

Setting her sack on the porch, Felicity slung her purse over her shoulder and marched across the thick, high grass toward the bordering estate. Aaron glanced up then ignored her. Even at a distance, Felicity saw the scowl marring his darkly tanned brow.

"I'll help you look for them," she said crisply, as soon as she drew within earshot. "When were they last seen?"

"Thanks, but we don't want your help," Aaron said. "Go on back and enjoy your grandmother's life savings."

"What?"

"You heard me." His smile was silky and dangerous—a strange expression on such a ruggedly carved face. "Mrs. Tucker told me how her granddaughter robbed her of her small savings account. That was why she couldn't afford to get that menace of a well covered."

Felicity started to refute that.

"A woman who'd steal from a helpless old lady is worse than a gold digger," he snapped. "Now get out of here. We have better things to do than waste time with the likes of you."

Felicity overcame her desire to do something violent to Aaron's shins. Even in her own stunned condition, she realized he was in a state of strong emotion that had nothing to do with her.

"Now listen, Mr. Whitaker—"

"*You* listen. I want you off my property. If I have to get a court order to keep you off, I'll do it. Now move it."

"The more people who help you look—" she began.

The very idea enraged him. "I don't need any help from the likes of you. Now get your skinny little fanny off my property before I really lose my temper."

Felicity had faced down too many hostile sales prospects in her former career as a traveling saleswoman to be intimidated by an overwrought dog owner. She produced a soothing smile. "Since you're obviously feeling less than reasonable at the moment, I'll just get on home. I'll keep my eye out for them and call you if I see or hear anything."

"Go away," Aaron fairly snarled.

"After all, two schnauzers should be easy to spot."

Aaron stared at her a moment. "Lady, you are one loony little nutcase. Get off my property before I put you on that silly-looking saddle of yours and ride you clean out of town."

Felicity smiled at the vision of herself riding the miniature saddle on her purse. The artisan had assured her it was correct in every detail.

"See you later, Mr. Whitaker. In the meantime, I'll keep an eye out for your dogs."

She turned on her heel and marched back across the thick, almost knee-high grass, ignoring Aaron's frustrated exclamation. She ruined the effect by tripping over a hidden crawfish mound and nearly falling flat on her face.

So much for being neighborly. Felicity reached her front porch once more and took notice of her damp, steamy state. She was only too happy to return to the air-conditioned comfort of her own place—except the air conditioner wasn't working, and the repairman wouldn't arrive until tomorrow. She inserted her key into the lock and wondered why a man desperate to find his dogs was so equally determined not to accept any help from her. It was downright puzzling.

Something was wrong with her key. Felicity pulled it out and gazed at the key tip. It was coated with a sticky, glue-like white substance. Worse, the door was unlocked. Felicity shoved it open with her booted-foot and glared inside. After tangling with Aaron, she felt primed to deal with a burglar.

She saw no one, but then she hadn't expected anyone. She had already discovered the front door lock was unreliable at best. Felicity registered another addition to her list of repairpersons to call and stalked inside.

Dumping her grocery sack and purse unceremoniously onto the welter of old newspapers and magazines littering the sofa, she turned back and studied the offending lock. The peculiar white substance was now oozing from the keyhole.

Pondering the matter, Felicity retrieved two more sacks of cleaning supplies from her truck and another sack full of boxes of large plastic trash bags. She glared across the expanse of grass. Aaron had crossed the road that ran before their houses and was searching the field opposite, where several dozen humped, mahogany-colored cows grazed peacefully.

To the rear of the Whitaker property, the slender dark-headed woman scurried frantically toward the barn and over to the equally distraught housekeeper. The two exchanged helpless gestures that aroused Felicity's sympathy. As soon as she changed her clothes, she was joining in the search whether Aaron liked it or not.

She threaded her way toward the bedroom. Her grandmother had saved every piece of paper that had crossed her path during the past five years and the stacks formed an obstacle course for the unwary.

The telephone shrilled. Felicity grimaced and detoured to the kitchen to answer it. The kitchen cabinets and one drawer stood open, revealing a collection of pans and utensils interspersed with miscellaneous junk.

"Hi, Mama," she said in patient tones. "Of course, I'm all right. What could possibly have happened to me in the two hours since I last talked to you?" She listened a moment. "Because I was at the grocery store buying gallon jugs of Mr. Clean and boxes and boxes of plastic trash bags, that's why. I told you I was going to the store. I'll get a new cell phone tomorrow."

While reassuring her mother that she hadn't been mugged in the grocery store parking lot, Felicity cast her gaze around the kitchen. Had those cabinet doors popped open on their own?

"Yes, Mama. Don't worry. I didn't realize there was no cell coverage for my phone here. I'll buy one tomorrow that has local coverage. In the meantime, this old landline still works fine."

When she hung up the phone, she became aware of a peculiar odor in the house. Sniffing curiously, Felicity arrived at the bedroom door. She didn't remember closing it, and it seemed a little difficult to push open.

The odor strengthened as the door swung open. Felicity stared toward the windows; the dusty window sills bore oval globs of a pearly-white substance. She looked down. An old towel had been rolled up and stuffed into the crack between the door and the floor. The small room was empty, but Felicity remained on the threshold, her scalp prickling. That odor had to be Elmer's Glue. Grandma Lureen had left several large bottles of the stuff scattered around the house.

Felicity studied every detail of the room. Someone had glued her windows shut. Suddenly, she was glad Aaron was nearby… surely, he'd come to her aid if she screamed.

Emboldened, Felicity stepped into the room. There were squiggly white lines of Elmer's Glue everywhere, as if someone had tried to seal up every crack in the floors or walls.

A muffled sneeze from the closet made her jump violently. She skittered back to the door, heart pounding madly. It took several seconds for Felicity's brain to shift into gear. She laid her hand on the doorknob, pulled open the closet door, and looked into the frightened faces of two small boys armed for battle.

Each child held a saucepan lid in front of him like a shield, and wore the pan as a helmet. The older boy held a long-handled fork in a menacing fashion, while the younger clutched a kitchen fork. Both seemed oddly relieved to see Felicity peering down at them.

Suddenly, it all made sense.

"Hello, Pete. Good afternoon, Joey." She smiled soothingly. "I'm glad the two of you came to pay me a visit, but why are you waiting in the closet?"

The older of the two boys, who couldn't have been more than five, met Felicity's friendly gaze with wide-eyed trust. "We're hiding," he said in a grave little voice.

"Yes, I can see that." Felicity blinked in surprise. "Your—" she wasn't sure whether they were Aaron's children or not, "—relatives are very worried because they can't find you. What are you hiding from?"

"The ghost." The younger boy scrunched closer to his brother. "The ghost might get us."

Great. On top of everything else, the house that was to be her temporary castle was haunted. Felicity sighed and mentally added "exorcist" to the list of repair people she was about to call.

"Welcome to Foxe, Felicity," she said aloud.

Chapter 2

Aaron hated to do it, but even he had to admit it was time to call the sheriff. Scowling ferociously, he headed back toward the house. His sister, Deborah Sachitano, ran to meet him.

Aaron deliberately wiped the scowl off his face, all too aware a frown was enough to frighten his gentle sister. Tears streamed down her face as she clutched his arm; tears which burned Aaron's heart. Her blue eyes beseeched him for information he couldn't give her.

"We can't find them anywhere. Oh, Aaron, do you think Tony could have taken them?"

"Now calm down, Deb," Aaron said, in spite of his own fears. "He won't take them while I'm around. He knows better."

Deborah gave a small gasp as she fought for control. "What are we going to do? If Tony didn't take them, and they didn't fall down Mrs. Tucker's old well, then where are they?"

It was natural for Deborah to lean on someone and just as natural for Aaron to lend support. Besides, taking care of Deborah was a long-established habit. He put an arm around her shoulders and gave her a quick hug.

"Let's search the house one more time, then I'll call Sheriff Darby," he said. "There's a chance the boys took off for a walk down the road."

"But they know they aren't supposed to leave the yard," Deborah said, trembling. "Did you ask the woman next door if she's seen them?"

"Remember, honey, she just got home," he said, schooling his voice into a soft rumble. "She couldn't possibly have seen them."

Aaron felt a twinge of remorse. He'd been so worried about his two missing nephews, and so frustrated at the sight of Felicity in her sexy western outfit, he hadn't asked.

He was well aware he was overreacting, but he had known Felicity Clayton was trouble the moment he laid eyes on her. Already angry because Joey had almost tumbled into the well barely two days ago, he was infuriated to realize Lureen's granddaughter drove a new truck and wore fashionable, expensive clothes.

He had watched from his bedroom window while she arrived at Lureen's house then spent the morning finding out all he could about her. When he happened to catch sight of her truck at the town's only large grocery store, he hadn't intended to lose his temper. But then again, he hadn't expected his own physical reaction to Felicity Clayton. Accustomed to being in control at all times, Aaron was doubly angry with himself for finding the woman attractive. Lureen had told him her granddaughter thought of nothing but money.

Aaron reminded himself that Felicity had stolen money from an elderly woman, her own grandmother. What was more, she was too skinny, with brown-and-brown rather than blue-and-blond as he preferred.

His sister gave a mighty sniff and brushed tears off her cheeks with shaking hands. "Up until last week, they used to walk next door with you every day to see how poor Mrs. Tucker was feeling. I just thought maybe…"

Aaron's antenna went up. He should have thought of that. "We'll go over there and ask right now. Barney Deshotel at the realtor's place says her name is Felicity Clayton, and that she's Mrs. Tucker's granddaughter." He kept his arm around his sister and guided her across the lawn toward Lureen's old house. The situation was too serious to allow prejudice to rule his good sense.

"She seems so…so animated," Deborah said hesitantly. "And so brave. Imagine staying all by herself in that spooky old house. And with all Mrs. Tucker's papers and things still in there."

He heard Deborah's unspoken desire to fear no man and no junked-up old house like the cheeky Miss Felicity Clayton. His heart was wrung. After all she had been through in her young life, and now this. Aaron cursed inwardly. He had sworn to protect his sister and her children. He had failed.

Barely one month ago, Deborah had left her husband, Tony Sachitano. During that time, scarcely a day had gone by without Tony calling and demanding to speak to his wife, insisting he'd done nothing and issuing ultimatums that she return home instantly. Aaron privately thought Tony might possibly kidnap his two sons in hopes of forcing Deborah to come back to him, but common sense told him that hadn't happened in this case. The dogs hadn't barked a warning and both Deborah and the housekeeper had seen nothing. The boys had simply vanished from sight, probably by means of their own little legs.

Aaron had always liked Tony and would have sworn he was a gentleman, but who really knew what went on between a man and his wife? Whatever had happened, Tony had no business terrorizing Deborah by kidnapping the children, and so Aaron would tell him if that turned out to be the case.

"I think I would like her, Aaron. Do you think—?" She broke off suddenly with a painful gasp.

"Do I think what, honey?" Aaron asked gently.

"It might be nice to invite her to your company barbecue tomorrow evening if—if..."

"Sure, honey. We'll ask her." Aaron frowned. The last thing he wanted was Felicity at the annual barbecue he threw for his employees and customers, but he would have agreed to anything that lifted Deborah's spirits. "And don't worry. We'll find the boys. I'll bet they caught a ride to Dairy Queen to spend that five-dollar bill I gave Pete this morning."

A shriek erupted from Deborah's lips; adrenaline shot through Aaron. He prepared to fight or give chase. Deborah tore from his grasp and raced ahead.

Aaron stared after her and saw the two small boys with Felicity. As they drew closer, Aaron saw that Felicity held each child's hand and that the children were wearing heavy armor and prepared for battle. If she thought she was going to get away with encouraging this sort of play with his nephews, she had better think again.

He thought longingly about lecturing her while his hands rested around her warm, slender neck. When his vision-self ended the lecture by dragging her against him for a kiss, Aaron knew he was in trouble.

He scowled heavily. It didn't help to realize he longed to take his frustration out on somebody capable of giving him a good fight. Aaron bit back a sudden grin. Perhaps he should invite her to dinner so they could both enjoy themselves by trading insults.

"I just thought I'd return your two missing schnauzers," Felicity called cheerfully. "They were hiding in a closet."

"Oh, thank you!" Deborah cried. "Thank you. Thank you. Joey, Pete, I told you never to leave Uncle Aaron's backyard." She reached her sons and fell to her knees, hugging them. "We were so worried about you."

Aaron smothered an exclamation of disgust with himself. He knew Lureen's front door lock was broken. She had told him so last month. But he never thought the boys would defy his orders and enter her house without permission. He stood behind Deborah, scowling and considering the best way to handle the situation. There was no question he owed the feisty Miss Clayton a debt of gratitude.

She must have read his mind. She tossed him a sassy smile that almost blinded him with its brilliance. "I'm lending them the helmets, shields, and swords for the night since I'll be eating out this evening. I'll need the energy, because it's going to take a while to get all the Elmer's Glue off the woodwork."

"Elmer's Glue?" Aaron was certain he'd missed something in the aftermath of that smile.

"Your schnauzers glued my bedroom windows shut. It seems Jason, whoever he is, told them a ghost can come through any little crack, so they tried to glue up all the cracks in my bedroom. That means the windows, the door, the keyhole, the woodwork, the floor planks…"

"What?" Aaron found himself totally baffled.

Deborah ceased kissing her sons' small faces to look up at Felicity through tear-filled, smiling blue eyes. "Jason is their cousin. He's a year older than Pete."

"Jason knows a lot about ghosts," Pete, the older boy, said. "They can come in through any hole, even a little bitty one."

"Honey, there are no such things as ghosts," Deborah said.

Three-year-old Joey waved the table fork. "I'll get that bad old ghost. I'll poke holes in him and let out all his air."

Aaron noted the carefully suppressed smile twitching Felicity's full mouth. He reminded himself this captivating woman had controlled poor old Lureen's house and bank account, refusing to give the old lady enough money for basic household repairs. If he didn't bear those things in mind, he might pay too much notice to those enchanting lips.

Before she died, Lureen had shared with him that Felicity refused to fix the lock on the front door. Therefore it was Felicity's fault that the boys had gotten inside.

"Why don't you ask your uncle for a garlic necklace?" Felicity asked.

Pete was all ears. "A garlic necklace?"

"Everyone knows a garlic necklace repels vampires, but not everyone knows it also repels ghosts." Felicity demonstrated with her hands, and Pete's unblinking blue gaze followed her gestures.

"Get a piece of garlic from the kitchen and hang it on a string around your neck. No ghost can touch a person who's wearing a garlic necklace."

Aaron stared, fascinated, at Felicity's highly visual demonstration of making a garlic necklace guaranteed to repel ghosts, vampires, and the evil eye.

Pete's face brightened. He tucked his fork into his waistband. "Let's go see Polly and get some garlic right now, Joey."

"Are you sure it won't let the ghost get us?" Joey asked.

"No ghost can get you with a garlic necklace around your neck," Felicity promised, with a wink. "By the way, Pete, why is this ghost after you?"

"I'm going to have a little talk with Jason," Deborah said sternly. "He has no business frightening the boys with nonsense like this."

Felicity smiled at Pete. "Did Jason tell you a ghost was after you?"

"No, ma'am." Pete looked trustfully up at her. "I heard Mama and Uncle Aaron talking."

Deborah gasped. "Why didn't you ask us what we were talking about, Pete? It certainly wasn't about any ghost."

Pete's blue eyes were wide and guileless. "I did ask you. You said it was private, between you and Uncle Aaron."

Aaron heard his sister's sudden intake of breath as he recalled the conversation in question. They had been discussing the possibility, in carefully couched terms, that Tony might kidnap his two sons in order to get his family back home again.

"Well, we certainly weren't talking about any ghost," Deborah said briskly. "There are no such things as ghosts."

"Jason says ghosts kill people." Joey, unconvinced, held his fork at the ready.

"Ghosts don't kill," Felicity said. "You can take my word for it. And no ghost will even come into a room where there's a garlic necklace."

"I'm going to call Jason's mother," Deborah promised.

Felicity said nothing, but her lively face spoke for her.

Aaron's fists clenched. The insolence of the woman. No doubt she blamed Deborah—and him—for intentionally creating the ghost in the children's minds. Before Aaron could set her straight, his housekeeper, Polly Fitzgerald, approached them at a run. Polly was a distant cousin, a middle-aged widow with no children, and she had become deeply attached to the boys during the past few weeks.

"Thank the good Lord," Polly cried. She arrived, panting, and promptly disguised her emotion with an air of exaggerated annoyance. "Now maybe I can get back to work. In case you folks have forgotten, we're giving a barbecue tomorrow."

"Do you have any garlic, Polly?" Pete asked.

Polly stared down at Pete's intense face then glanced at her employer. "Of course I have garlic. I keep it so I can make that chicken cacciatore your daddy likes."

Deborah's face paled, and Aaron frowned his disapproval at Polly. In spite of everything, Polly persisted in thinking the best of Tony.

"You boys get on back to the house," Aaron said. "I had better help restore Miss Clayton's house to normal."

"Actually, I believe Elmer's Glue responds to soap and water," Felicity said, with cheerful optimism. "It'll probably come up when I scrub."

"I'd better have a look at the damages just in case." Aaron wasn't a man to shirk his responsibilities. "Two little boys have ways of doing unintended damage."

Deborah's eyes followed her sons as they headed with Polly toward the house. "I'd better come too, Aaron. There's no telling what they've done."

"I'll take care of everything," Aaron said in his most soothing tones. "You go on back to the house and keep an eye on those two young devils."

Felicity smiled at Deborah. "You'd better go talk to them right now about what they overheard. Otherwise, they'll keep on being afraid to go to bed at night."

"I'll talk to them as soon as I get back," Aaron said. "Go on back to the house, Deb. I'll be there as soon as I've seen for myself what they did to Miss Clayton's window sills."

"I'm so sorry, Miss Clayton," Deborah said, stretching out her hands to Felicity. "If they did any permanent damage, of course I'll take care of it. And thank you so much for bringing them back immediately. I was absolutely petrified—" She broke off, unable to continue.

"Please call me Felicity." She clasped both of Deborah's hands, smiling warmly. "I doubt Elmer's Glue constitutes much of a threat to the woodwork. Besides, I enjoyed meeting your sons. They're very intelligent, handsome young men."

Aaron observed with disgust that Deborah was thoroughly won over. Felicity seemed to have a knack for getting on everyone's good side. Everyone, that is, except him. He knew too much about her to be taken in by that warm, friendly manner.

"And please come to the barbecue we're throwing tomorrow evening," Deborah said. "My boys would love to show you around, wouldn't they, Aaron?"

Aaron managed to second the invitation, although it went sorely against the grain with him.

Thankfully, Felicity waited until Deborah was out of earshot before firing the opening salvo in their battle.

"If you aren't careful, you'll just reinforce the ghost idea in those two little boys' heads," she said.

"And what makes you an expert?" How dare this woman tell him how to run his household? "I'll have you know—"

"I think you'd better hear some of the things they were telling me," Felicity interrupted. "They think this ghost is punishing them because they were bad. That's why their mother fled their own house to bring them here, and why their father hasn't come to get them yet. They believe the bad ghost is what's keeping their father away."

Aaron's fists clenched with a mixture of irritation with himself and fury at Felicity for pointing out his failings so starkly. He should have insisted that he and Deborah sit down with the boys and explain why they were staying with Uncle Aaron for a while, and why their father wouldn't be coming to visit anytime soon.

Instead, he had let Deborah talk him out of it, and now look at the result.

Felicity put her fists on her hips. "Pardon me for meddling in what obviously isn't my business, but you can't allow those children to live in fear like this."

He knew Felicity was right, but his need to protect Deborah was too strong. He hadn't insisted when Deborah begged him to say nothing to the boys about uprooting them from their home.

"Miss Clayton, my dealings with my nephews are not your concern," Aaron said, through clenched teeth. "As you pointed out, this situation is none of your business."

"Really?" Felicity inquired brightly. "In that case, I'd better go speak to your sister about the matter myself. And present her with a bill for the housecleaning fees."

She was deliberately provoking him, Aaron realized. For some reason, that put heart into him.

Felicity smiled sweetly and heaped fuel onto the burning fire within him. "If there's one thing I can spot a mile away, it's a tendency to be overprotective."

"You have a lot of nerve, you phony cowgirl," Aaron exploded. "You never paid one bit of attention to your grandmother while she was alive, but the minute she dies, you swoop in like a vulture to take what few pennies she had."

"If that's what you think, it's no wonder your nephews are having such problems," Felicity tossed back. "You'd believe anything anyone told you, no matter how nutty it was."

Aaron suppressed a twinge of caution. To be fair, Lureen was a real nutcase, what with her ridiculous political opinions and the signs she made and posted in front of her house or carried in front of businesses—but she'd been harmless.

"I checked on the deed to this house myself," he snapped, infuriated that he'd let Felicity's comment get to him. "It was in your name."

"Is that right?" Her small smile riled him further. "It's a pity you didn't check on a few other things while you were at it."

"Like what?" Aaron roared. It felt wonderful to rip into a worthy opponent at last. "The only thing I'd have found out is how much money you were lifting from that poor old lady's bank account."

"Or how much I was putting in?" Felicity asked, marvelously unaffected. "Do you know what your trouble is? You've jumped to a conclusion based on some half-baked facts, and now you're trying to scare me into agreeing with you. I have just one question: What do you do when you find out you're dead wrong?"

"I've never been wrong."

Aaron couldn't believe he heard himself shout such an enormous untruth. That just went to show how unaccustomed he was to giving way like this.

"Oh, brother." Felicity crossed her arms across her breasts and tilted her chin at a challenging angle. "Well, you may have scared everyone else around here into believing that whopper, but I'm immune to your scintillating charm."

"I'm not wrong about what you did to that poor old lady. You're a buzzard of the worst sort, cowgirl. A man would have to be a condor to deal with the likes of you."

Felicity's silver-banded teeth flashed at him in a grin of genuine amusement. "In that case, you're in serious trouble, because you aren't a condor. You're a cardinal."

"A what?" He reeled mentally, more off-balance than he'd ever been in dealing with a woman.

"The male cardinal is a very family-oriented bird," she informed him. "He often feeds other nests of baby birds besides his own." She nodded briskly in the face of his open-mouthed stare. "If ever I saw a human male who resembles a male cardinal, you're the one."

Aaron boiled with emotion. Chief among the mix of feelings was the certainty that this woman had seen straight through him and knew exactly what sort of man he was in spite of the tough outer shell he so carefully cultivated.

"If ever I saw a female buzzard, you're it. Let's get this over with, cowgirl. I haven't got all day."

"Sure you have," Felicity taunted. "That's what your problem is. You've got all day for anyone who needs you."

Once more Aaron had the uncomfortable sensation that he'd been seen through. "You know all about it, I'm sure." He abandoned the fiery rage for icy precision.

"As a matter of fact, I do. All my life I've suffered from an overprotective caretaker. Believe me, I know one when I see one." She smiled, and Aaron's gaze focused on her lips as they parted to reveal the silver bands on her teeth.

"Your vision wouldn't be obstructed, would it?" He scowled at her in the way that made his employees quake in their cowboy boots.

He wondered what the braces would feel like beneath the softness of her lips if he were to kiss her. The thought increased the intensity of his frown.

Felicity wasn't noticeably impressed by the famous Whitaker scowl.

"My optometrist says I've got perfect vision," she assured him. "As for my woodwork, don't worry your head, Mr. Whitaker. I'm counting on soap and water to take care of the problem."

"Nevertheless, I'd better see my nephews' damages for myself," Aaron said.

He couldn't help the surge of pleasure he felt at her total unconcern. These days, there were only a few people in town who didn't fear him.

Felicity looked at him thoughtfully. "I don't think I want you in my house. You might take it into your head that I need protecting from a mouse or something."

"The only thing you'll need protection from in Mrs. Tucker's house is a cockroach," Aaron said silkily. "Let's go, Miss Clayton. I need to get back."

"Ah, yes. The big barbecue. Your nephews are convinced the ghost will snatch them bodily out of the crowd. Maybe you should hire a special ghost-busting bodyguard."

"Someone such as yourself, Miss Clayton?"

Felicity tossed him a glance of contempt. "I've already done my part with the garlic necklaces. Excuse me, please. I'd better tackle that glue while it's still in a liquid state. Get lost, Mr. Whitaker."

She turned and marched through the tall grass toward her house, outrage in every line of her slim body. When his boots clattered on the wooden porch behind her, she whirled to confront him.

"I said get lost, Mr. Whitaker."

"I said I was coming in to assess the damages, and that's exactly what I'm going to do." Aaron gave her the stare that never failed to make secretaries hop and car salesmen quail.

"Well, I don't want you to. Now buzz off before I call the sheriff and tell him you're harassing me." She wrestled in vain with the doorknob. "Great. Now the lock has decided to work."

"Here," he said. "Allow me. Mrs. Tucker showed me the intricacies of this excuse for a lock some time ago."

He took the doorknob, rattled it expertly, and pounded the exact center of the door. It flew open.

"Unfortunately, someone had written a check that drew down her account and the landlord refused to pay for a locksmith." Aaron went on. "She was left with only twenty dollars left to live on until her next check came in."

"Is that right?"

"Have you always considered your grandmother's bank account yours to draw on, cowgirl?"

"What difference does it make to you?" She led the way inside. "They put glue in the keyhole, too. According to Pete, the living room is too full of cracks. That's why they opted to hide in the bedroom. It impressed them as being a little more snug."

The telephone shrilled.

"The bedroom is to the right down this hall. Go ahead and assess the damages while I catch that." She stalked to the kitchen and picked up the receiver. "Yes, Mama?"

She glanced up irritably when Aaron, curious, followed her to the kitchen. He looked around and pretended to be studying the mess.

"No, Mama, I haven't had time to look for them. Listen, I can't talk now. I have the exterminator here. Yes, I'll look through every single magazine if I have to. If they're here, I'll find them. I promise."

Aaron brushed by her to bend and peer in the junky cabinets, where his two nephews had rummaged in their efforts to arm themselves. Perhaps he ought to live up to her billing and stomp on the big cockroach that ran across the floor.

"What? Of course I'm safe. Why shouldn't I be? No, Mama. The exterminator is not likely to do me a meanness. He's a very sweet little man, barely five feet tall. I'll call you back in a few minutes, okay? I have to get his estimate."

Aaron bit back a grin. She hadn't been lying when she said she had an overprotective relative. How she managed to escape her mother to travel to Foxe, he had no idea.

Aaron discovered an old plastic radio buried beneath the political magazines on the kitchen counter and switched it on. The sound of Becky Lozano's clear voice singing her recent hit filled the small room: "…protectin' my baby from that adventuresome spirit…"

Felicity winced.

Aaron switched off the radio. "What an exciting life you must lead. For your mother to worry this much about you…" His voice trailed off suggestively.

"Come this way, Mr. Whitaker. I've got better things to do than entertain you."

"Things like looking for the keys to that old lady's safe deposit box?" He followed her back to the living room.

"If she has one, it'll sure take some searching to find the keys," Felicity said. "As you can see, my grandmother was something of a pack rat."

"Better that than other things she might have been." Aaron paused a moment for emphasis. "I suppose it's a case of 'like mother, like daughter.'"

Felicity glanced back at him, forehead wrinkled in puzzlement. "I don't think—"

"According to Mrs. Tucker, you're just like your mother."

Her eyes went wide. She turned to stare at him, but any satisfaction he might have felt at hitting the nail on the head was vanquished when Felicity broke into unabashed, full-throated laughter. She collapsed on the sofa, still laughing.

Aaron couldn't figure it out. "Lady, you *are* a nutcase."

Felicity nodded in a solemn manner. "What can I say? It's an inherited condition."

Chapter 3

"Felicity," Pete called. "Let's go look at the cow."

Felicity could think of many things she'd rather look at than a whole, butchered cow turning over a huge bed of red coals. She had never attended a genuine Texas barbecue before, and she would think twice before attending another.

For one thing, the humid evening air was heavier than ever with the odor of mesquite smoke, roasting beef, and the ubiquitous little black bugs. For another, Whitaker Chevrolet had provided entertainment in the form of a country band with a predilection for Becky Lozano songs.

Worse, Felicity could hardly keep her eyes off Whitaker Chevrolet's CEO. Aaron looked like a cowboy straight out of a western movie—tall, dark, and formidable. He wore a black western shirt bejeweled with silver buttons, and his broad shoulders were decorated with fringe that swung when he moved. His long, muscular legs were encased in black jeans and boots that attracted many feminine glances.

She reminded herself she was here for business purposes, not to admire Aaron's appearance. She followed Pete and Joey across the lawn, through the milling crowd toward the barbecue pit. Strings of lights hanging overhead gave the evening scene a peculiar daylight quality.

"You're with Aaron Whitaker, right?" a woman asked. "I just love your outfits. The two of you are dressed just like Roy Rogers and Dale Evans in one of the movies I saw when I was a kid."

"Actually, I'm a friend of the Sachitano family," Felicity returned, indicating Pete and Joey. "Felicity Clayton. I'm just visiting for a few weeks. If you like what I'm wearing and ever make it to

Nashville, tell the ladies at the Cosmic Cowgirl Boutique you're a personal friend of mine. Or you can shop the online store at the web address on the card."

She produced a business card. Who knew when one of the women at the barbecue might travel through Nashville and stop in at the boutique or shop online? That was the only reason she had decided to accept Aaron's grudging invitation to attend the Whitaker Chevrolet Barbecue, she reminded herself.

After all, who knew how long she'd have to stay in Foxe, Texas, away from the Cosmic Cowgirl? If she could drum up some new customers while she was here, the trip wouldn't be totally wasted.

Regarding the barbecue as an opportunity to show off her wares, Felicity donned a pair of form-fitting white jeans and a fringed yellow western shirt. Golden, long-horned cattle earrings swung from her ears. Her unruly mass of brown hair had been pulled back and snagged with yellow combs.

Interest in her business ran high; but curiosity over who she was—and whether she was Aaron's lover—proved higher. Felicity muttered imprecations to herself, but there wasn't a thing she could do about it.

"Welcome, folks, to the annual Whitaker Chevrolet Texas Barbecue," the master of ceremonies intoned. "Miss Ruthie Fisher will sing in honor of the occasion."

Ruthie, a buxom blonde, burst into "Telephone Trouble,"—a Becky Lozano song about a long wrangle with the telephone company and the Nashville police department one night when her beloved one's telephone had been out of order. The song seemed to catalog a woman's fears about being unable to talk with her lover, but careful attention to the lyrics revealed that the singer was actually trying to call her daughter.

Felicity decided to leave the moment they served the barbecue.

She held the little boys' hands tightly to keep them from getting too close to the barbecue pit. The roasting beef smelled delicious, but Felicity figured she could do without having an actual plate of the stuff.

"You're new in town, aren't you?" a man said, stepping in front of her. "Are you planning on opening a business here?"

Felicity recognized him as the master of ceremonies. Since almost everyone here was somehow related to Whitaker Chevrolet, she pegged him immediately as a car salesman, early forties, and probably newly divorced.

"I'm Grover Madison. You look like a sharp businesswoman," he said. "Let's sit down and talk a while."

"She's a little young for you, Grover," Aaron said from behind them. "Why don't you run along and speak to Mrs. Junker? I understand she's in the market for a new Chevrolet."

Felicity bared her brightly-banded teeth at Aaron. "I turned eighteen this morning, Grandpa."

Grover's pale blue eyes started. He gulped visibly and squeaked, "Eighteen?"

"Give or take a few years." Felicity gave Aaron a challenging glance then returned her attention to Grover. "You're helping to organize the Rice Festival this year, aren't you? I'm really looking forward to seeing Randy MacElroy perform."

Grover quickly started to resemble a nervous guppy. He stared from Aaron to Felicity.

"Is the barbecue done yet, Felicity?" Joey tugged at her hand.

"It'll be ready in a few minutes." Aaron bent to lift Joey into his arms. "What do you say we show Miss Clayton your ponies?"

"Oh, boy." Pete hopped on one foot. "Uncle Aaron gave us horses, Felicity. Mine is named Donatello and Joey's is Michelangelo."

Felicity reached for Pete's hand. "I'd love to see them." She smiled at Grover. "Maybe we'll have a chance to talk later this evening."

"Grover is going to be busy," Aaron said smoothly. "As master of ceremonies, it's his duty to circulate and make sure the guests are having a good time."

The pointed statement wasn't lost on Grover. "I was looking for you, Aaron. We got word this afternoon that Randy MacElroy canceled out on us, but boy, did we ever luck out with our celebrity entertainer this year."

Grover took on such an air of self-importance that Felicity wondered why Aaron didn't kick him.

"Randy canceled?" She frowned. "He'd never—I mean Randy wouldn't cancel a concert unless something awful happened."

Before she could ask what was wrong with Randy, Ruthie Fisher appeared and gave Aaron an enticing smile. Her fringed blue satin shirt gaped open at the neck to reveal a considerable amount of tanned cleavage.

"Aaron, sugar, why don't you come up here and sing a couple for the folks? Hi, honey," Ruthie said to Felicity. She entwined her arm through Aaron's. "That's a fantastic outfit you're wearing. Wish I was that skinny."

Felicity smiled, realizing Ruthie meant the words as a compliment. "It's my genetic code. My mother says I ought to eat and be grateful."

"Oh, honey, I sure would." Ruthie beamed and tugged at Aaron's arm. "Come on up, sugar. The fans are waiting."

"You go ahead, Mr. Whitaker, sugar," Felicity sassed. "The boys and I will go see the horses."

To his credit, Aaron didn't look particularly eager to mount the platform beside Ruthie, but he went gracefully enough. From the reaction of the crowd, they looked forward to this part of the entertainment every year.

Aaron's smooth, deep tones floated out over the crowd. His words took on a warmth and depth that his rough-speaking voice lacked. If he had been any other man, Felicity might have stayed and listened. Instead, she followed the two little boys to the buffet table, grabbed a few apple slices, and fled.

She breathed in the fragrant, hay-scented air of the stable and followed the boys down the wide, concrete hall. Sounds of horses replaced the smooth sound of Aaron's voice, and Felicity suppressed a twinge of nervousness. If it came to horses versus Aaron Whitaker, the horses were a much safer bet.

He was very good—too good. A man with a voice like that was bound to have dreams of stardom. Felicity shuddered. Thank goodness she'd found out before her unwilling attraction to him had time to grow. She loved country music, but she had plenty of reasons to avoid would-be country musicians.

"Donatello likes apples," Pete said. "Look, Felicity."

She approached cautiously and peered over the stall door. Donatello was a small pony whose head was no taller than Felicity's shoulder. Rather than dance about nervously, the pony stood sedately while Pete stroked its neck. Felicity relaxed a little. She also had plenty of reasons to avoid horses, but on the whole, she'd rather avoid Aaron than his horses.

"So he does," she said. "Does your father like horses?"

"My daddy says we live in the city, so we can't have a horse." Pete fed the pony another apple slice.

"When is my daddy coming?" Joey came to stand before Felicity. "I want him. When is he coming?"

"I don't know, sweetheart." No wonder they invented ghosts to be afraid of, Felicity decided. Whatever had happened between their parents hadn't made them fear their father. "What does your mother say?"

Joey's big, blue eyes filled with tears, and his lower lip quivered. "She says she doesn't know. Why doesn't she know?"

Felicity looked at Pete. He looked back at her with trust and expectation.

"I'm sure you'll see him soon," she compromised. "He must miss you both. Do you think Michelangelo would take an apple from me?"

Fortunately, the children were young enough to be easily distracted. Felicity gingerly held out a slice as the boys watched eagerly, then jerked her hand back when the pony's soft muzzle brushed her skin.

"He won't bite," Pete assured her.

"I can see he's a very well-mannered horse." Joey's Michelangelo was an even smaller pony than Donatello, but a horse was a horse to Felicity.

"Will you take us riding, Felicity?" Pete asked. "You're a good cowgirl."

"Yes," Joey echoed, bouncing happily at the thought.

Felicity gulped. Here was where image ran head-on into reality and collapsed. "I don't have a horse of my own here. Maybe later, when I've had time to...er...get one."

She had always gone by the adage that image was everything. But here was a case where it really would be nice if she had at least one cowgirl-related skill.

"Uncle Aaron has lots of horses," Pete assured her. "He'll let you ride one."

"Well, uh...," Felicity began.

"Please, Felicity," Joey begged. "We want you to."

"She'll be happy to, won't you, Felicity?" Aaron's familiar, gravelly voice spoke up.

She might have known he'd turn up at exactly the wrong time. Felicity glanced irritably over her shoulder. Aaron seemed twice as intimidating in his black western outfit.

"As I was explaining, I don't have a horse."

"I've got horses." Aaron leaned his shoulder against the wall and propped one booted foot against the stall door. "Lots of horses."

"Well, I don't, and I make it a point never to ride someone else's horse."

Aaron's lazy smile transformed his entire face. "Come along and take your pick."

"I'm very busy tomorrow," Felicity said. "I have the carpenter coming out and an electrician."

"Here's a beauty." Ignoring her speech, Aaron walked a few steps and gestured toward a stall. "What do you think?"

Felicity looked and suppressed a shudder. The animal stood at least five or six feet high at the shoulder, and it looked like a mass of quivering flesh and adrenalin. She just knew the horse was aching to bolt, or stomp, or bite, or buck her off if she was stupid enough to mount him.

"It's lovely," she said. "But—"

"It's a she." Aaron rubbed the horse's muzzle and presented an apple sliver Pete handed him. "She's a real lady, aren't you, Quiche?"

Felicity observed the large, square teeth crunching the apple sliver. The horse looked like a biter; lady or no.

"Felicity can race us to the pond," Pete said.

Joey concurred, hopping up and down with excitement.

"I see what the problem is." Aaron gestured briskly. "You'd like a more spirited horse than Quiche."

He reached for her arm and led her a few stalls down. Felicity ignored the warmth of his big hand and sought to plant her boots on the concrete.

"Rhyolite is my favorite," Aaron said.

The sight of Rhyolite reduced Felicity to a state of paralysis. She stared, dry-mouthed, at the huge, gray horse.

"Well?" Aaron clearly expected some sort of praise from her.

"It's—" She cleared her throat. "It's a beautiful horse. Excuse me, please. I'd better be going; I'm expecting a telephone call."

"No." Joey's little face crumpled.

"You can't go yet." Pete grabbed her hand. "We haven't had any barbecue."

"Is this another telephone call from your mother?" Aaron asked, grinning. He indicated the horse. "'It' is a gelding, which makes him a he. He's yours for tomorrow afternoon. And my nephews are right. You can't leave yet."

Felicity had no idea what a gelding was, but she was determined to bluff her way through it. "I can see perfectly well he's a gelding, but I'm not about to ride your horse," she said. "Let's go have some barbecue, boys. I'll have to be leaving in a few minutes."

"Hold on a minute." Aaron indicated the big, gray gelding and the chestnut mare down the row. "Are you saying you'd rather ride Quiche?"

She felt sure Aaron was setting her up for something. For once, her usual composure deserted her.

"No. You'd better ride Rhyolite," he said. "You're a woman who likes a challenge. I knew that the minute I saw you."

"Is that right?" Now Felicity knew she was being set up. "Hush, boys. Thank you, Mr. Whitaker, but I'm too busy right now to take time off for riding." She grabbed for Joey's hand. "Now what do you say we go get some of that good barbecue?"

Pete was brave but despairing. Joey, however, was heartbroken and didn't care who knew it.

"Pete, take Joey and make sure Michelangelo and Donatello are comfortable for the night," Aaron said. "Remember how I taught you to brush them?"

Pete and Joey disappeared with dragging steps into the two small stalls, and Aaron turned to Felicity. "Well, Miss Clayton, are you going to give in gracefully?"

Felicity regarded him warily. "What do you mean?"

He gave her a silky smile. "A cowgirl such as yourself is bound to be an expert rider. I know you wouldn't want to disappoint two little boys. Especially two little boys undergoing a lot of emotional upheaval."

"Oh, well, I—"

"In fact, I feel I'm insulting you by offering you two such gentle mounts," he pursued.

"As a matter of fact, I—"

"But the boys and I will see to it that you get plenty of exercise. Just be ready at five, will you?"

"I told you, I—"

"And don't tell me you don't ride," he interrupted. "Your image as an intrepid cowgirl would be ruined if you turn out to be a phony who can't ride a horse."

Felicity glared. "Of course I ride. Don't draw any conclusions just because I don't care to go riding with you."

"Now, honey," he said, grinning wickedly, "you aren't going riding with me. You're going riding with the boys. I'll just be along for the exercise."

Felicity drew in her breath and gritted her teeth. "Thanks for the *wonderful* opportunity to prove myself a real cowgirl, but—"

"Rhyolite has been trained for jumping."

Jumping? Felicity paled.

"Mr. Whitaker, I do not wish to go riding with you."

"Yes, Miss Clayton, you do. You wouldn't want the boys to tell everyone you can't ride a horse, would you?"

The guileless smile that accompanied this speech made Felicity long to wipe it off his face by saddling Rhyolite and jumping six fences.

"Whether or not I'm able to ride a horse has nothing to do with it," she snapped. "The fact that I do not wish to ride with you does."

"Oh, come now, Miss Clayton." Aaron gave her a lazy smile. "Surely you understand that, for the time being, where my nephews go, I go. And they want to go with you."

Felicity swallowed. How hard could it be to ride a horse? "Of course I understand, Mr. Whitaker. I'm the object of an overprotective relative myself."

"Ah, yes," Aaron said. "The telephone call you're expecting. Well, Miss Clayton, let's feed you a good plate of barbecue and send you on home to receive your mother's nightly phone call. How old did you say you were?"

"Twenty-six going on six as far as my mother is concerned," Felicity returned. "The thing is she's upset because I've come way down here for a few weeks. She thinks rural Texans such as yourself are savages." She added thoughtfully, "I'm not so sure she doesn't have a point there."

"I'm a very civilized savage," Aaron said, grinning. "I'd never disappoint my nephews; Rhyolite it is."

Felicity didn't like the way he said that. She looked again at Rhyolite. How difficult could it be to sit astride a horse and let it carry her around? She'd show Aaron Whitaker a thing or two. All she had to do was perfect some method of staying in the saddle. Say, super glue on the seat of her pants.

"Then certainly I'll ride Rhyolite." She hoped she sounded gracious rather than peeved. "I wouldn't disappoint the boys for the world. Now, if you'll excuse me, I've got to be going."

Not ready to end the conversation, Aaron moved to block her. The way Pete and Joey took everything Felicity said to heart made Aaron wonder if the woman was such a skilled manipulator of men, she could entrap them at any age. He warned himself to arm his heart against her.

Maybe it was already too late. He stared at her slender face, large brown eyes, and full, sensuous lips. She wasn't even his type, but he couldn't wait to kiss her.

"Will you please move?" She glared up at him, eyes flashing nervously.

"Now, Miss Clayton, calm down." He took her arm and walked her down the long hall, stopping before another stall. "You haven't seen the rest of my horses, yet. This is Tornado, the stallion I just bought."

He had never seen anything quite as peculiar as the look Felicity gave Tornado. Torn between laughter and an aching desire to kiss her, Aaron forced himself to drop her arm.

"Wonderful," she said, with a complete lack of enthusiasm for the highly-bred quarter horse.

"He's still a little nervous of the new surroundings."

"Is that right?" Felicity muttered.

The stallion pawed the floor, tossed his head, bared his teeth, and twitched his tail. Aaron could have sworn Felicity backed up an inch at every twitch. In fact, she was backing steadily into him, oblivious of the fact that he stood directly behind her.

Far be it for him to disappoint a woman who had found a new and interesting way to get him to kiss her. Aaron put his hands at her waist and turned her to face him.

Her fixed, blank expression meant nothing to Aaron. He answered her invitation and pulled her into his arms. She felt sleek and perfect, and her tangy scent lingered in his nostrils.

He'd never experienced anything like her mouth. To his fascination, he discovered that braces altered the way his mouth fit over hers. Definitely, braces altered the texture of her lips.

"Mmmmmmmphhh," Felicity said.

Aaron ignored her protest. He felt her hands come up around his shoulders, but he was busy exploring the rough feel of her braces with his tongue.

The braces enticed him. Slipping his tongue between her upper lip and her teeth, he stroked the gleaming metal bands and the smooth enamel of her teeth, experiencing the contrasts and finding them doubly fascinating.

He had never held a woman as slender as Felicity before. The feel of her willowy strength in his arms set his blood on fire. In fact, he was so interested in the perfect way she fit into his arms that it took him a moment to register the rap of her boot heel on his instep.

"Ouch! What was that for?" he demanded.

Felicity whisked herself out of his arms the moment they loosened. "That was for excessive handling of the merchandise. Careful, Mr. Whitaker, you might wind up having to make an unexpected purchase."

Aaron let out a sharp crack of appreciative laughter.

"Not me, sweetheart. I'm very careful where I buy."

"That's open for debate."

"Felicity, come see Michelangelo," Pete called from a stall down the stable aisle. "I just brushed him so he'll look pretty for our ride tomorrow."

"I'd better do the same to Rhyolite," Aaron said. "Otherwise, he'll have a hard time competing with those fancy cowgirl outfits of yours."

Felicity viewed Michelangelo's shining coat. Aaron noted the resigned expression on her face and grinned inwardly. She was skilled at manipulation. He had to hand it to her. Even though he knew she had probably achieved her object in getting him to kiss her, she didn't seem the least bit interested in her success.

If he hadn't known better, he'd have been piqued.

She remained thoughtful and largely silent when he escorted her back to the barbecue and seated her at a picnic table between the two boys with a plate of his excellent barbecue. Deborah sat across from them, smiling and at ease. Felicity appeared to have a list of items stored in her brain that enabled her to strike up a conversation with anyone.

For the second time that evening, he had to cut off his recently divorced new-car salesman, Grover Madison, who bore down on

Felicity with the look of a man who had staked out new territory. Grover didn't need to be chasing a woman like Felicity unless he planned on selling her a new car, and so Aaron intended to tell him, first thing Monday morning.

"How's the barbecue, Miss Clayton?" Aaron asked. "Is it done to your standards?"

He sat down opposite her, enjoying the way she glanced up then deliberately looked back down at her plate.

"The barbecue is perfect, thank you." She nibbled a bite of the succulent beef. "You sing very well. Have you ever thought about singing professionally?"

Aaron flashed her a pleased grin. She hadn't been as disinterested as he'd thought.

"I spent a few years playing every honky-tonk in Nashville, but I sounded too much like Johnny Cash," he said. "About the time I wised up and developed my own style, my uncle asked me to come here and take over the car dealership."

"You were happy to leave, I suppose."

"As a matter of fact, I was." He studied her, puzzled by something in her attitude. "I decided life on the road wasn't for me. It can be pretty rough, you know."

"Is that right?" Felicity delved into her barbecue.

"You sound as though you don't believe me," Aaron said. "Why not?"

Felicity looked up. "Why shouldn't I believe you?"

"That's what I'd like to know." Aaron watched the expression in her wide, brown eyes. "Most women are fascinated with the struggles of wannabe country singers."

"And I'm not?" Felicity shrugged. "I guess I prefer the genuine article."

There was a beat of silence, then Aaron threw back his head and roared with laughter. "How many genuine articles do you know, Miss Clayton?"

"She lives in Nashville, Aaron," Deborah said. "Naturally she must see a lot of country stars."

"She's right." Felicity's lips curved irrepressibly into a grin. "It so happens I know dozens of country singers."

"In that case, how about taking a turn on the stage?"

"Sorry. Your guests would get sick and run home. With any luck, they'd blame it on the barbecue and tell the police you tried to poison them."

"Are you trying to tell me you can't sing?"

"I'm absolutely tone deaf." She shrugged. "My mother can't understand it. She's had two voice coaches check me out, and they both agree I can't carry a tune."

Aaron broke into fresh laughter. Of all the replies he might have expected, that hadn't been one of them.

"Felicity can too sing." Joey frowned across the table at his uncle. "Felicity can do anything."

"I sing only to people who love me." Felicity smiled tenderly at the little boy. "They're the only people who can stand my singing."

On stage, Ruthie Fisher launched into "Protecting My Baby," Becky Lozano's current hit.

"Are you all right?" Aaron asked quietly. "Do you have a headache?"

"As a matter of fact, I do." She rubbed her forehead.

"Do Becky Lozano songs always affect you like this?"

Felicity stared at him, shocked.

"This is the second time I've seen you actually cringe, and each time, Becky Lozano was playing."

"It isn't Becky Lozano," she said, at last. "It's the song."

"'Protecting My Baby?'" Aaron listened to the song a moment then grinned sympathetically. "I see. Everyone thinks Becky is singing about her lover, but it's actually the song of a mother whose child is growing up. Reminds you of home, I suppose."

Felicity nodded, and a faint, wry smile played across her full mouth. "You're right. I quit liking the song as soon as I listened closely to the words."

"Exactly." Aaron cut a piece of barbecue from the bone for Joey and transferred it to the little boy's plate. "Are you otherwise a fan of Becky Lozano, Miss Clayton?"

"As a matter of fact, I am."

"In that case, you'll be interested in the news Grover is about to announce."

Felicity froze. "You don't mean…?"

"That's right." Aaron nodded, inordinately pleased with her expression of blank astonishment. "Becky Lozano has accepted a last minute invitation to fill in as our celebrity entertainer at the Rice Festival this year. Would you like a chance to meet her?"

A moment later, Felicity recovered her poise. "Thanks, but I'll probably give the festival a miss." She fastened her gaze on her plate. "Besides, I've already met Ms. Lozano."

Chapter 4

"Mama, how could you do this to me?" Felicity cried into the telephone receiver. "You said you weren't going to come near this town until I've had a chance to get this house into better condition."

The telephone had summoned her as she walked in her front door. Knowing who was on the other end of the line heightened Felicity's sense of injury, not to mention her headache.

"Now, darlin'." Becky Lozano's lilting Kentucky accent always grew extremely pronounced when she performed. When it came to explaining her actions to her daughter, she was definitely on stage. "Surely you don't expect your mama to stay away from her little girl for weeks and weeks. When Randy couldn't make the show, I just thought to myself, I thought, Becky, you could do that show, and you could see your baby at the same time."

"Don't hand me that," Felicity grumbled. "I know you made some sort of deal with Randy."

Becky laughed warmly. "Well, honey, what else could I do? I needed an excuse, didn't I? It's been at least two weeks since I've kissed your pretty face."

As always, Becky's heavy use of honeyed words slipped past Felicity's mental barricades. She collapsed on one of the rickety kitchen chairs, and groaned in protest.

Being a famous singer who was often separated from her daughter didn't mean Becky Lozano wasn't a mother tigress who would die for her cub. Three different cellular telephone companies made fortunes off Becky, and Becky's daughter usually felt as if her mother was in the next room, even if she was actually on her tour bus on the other side of the continent.

Felicity rubbed her aching forehead and wondered what it was about her vacation in Texas that sent Becky into a spasm of motherly anxiety. After all, Becky was in Texas about as often as she was in Tennessee, especially now that her career had finally blossomed.

"Now, sugar," Becky said in brisk tones, "just you calm your little self down and listen to your mama. In a couple of weeks, you'll have that house cleaned out, right? Your mama is coming, baby. You and me can have a grand old time just visiting and talking girl talk." She added on a practical note, "We can tie my appearance in with the Cosmic Cowgirl Boutique. Everybody can come look at my clothes and get an autograph and a business card. Who's more cowgirl than a country-western singer?"

The businesswoman in Felicity acknowledged the selling power of a Becky Lozano personal appearance and the attendant print interviews, but this was a case where she'd like to be long gone before anybody found out she was Becky's daughter. At the same time, Felicity didn't have it in her to deny her mother the comfort of being able to see her whenever Becky felt the need.

"All right, Mama," she said, resigned to the fact of her own soft-heartedness. "I'd better get some posters made, advertising the boutique and our web site. Maybe that picture of you in the fringed buckskin outfit—"

Becky shrieked. "Everyone'll think I'm a hundred years old. You just wait, sugar. I'll get Chester to send you one of the new shots. I look twenty, I promise you."

"Great, Mama," Felicity said automatically. She rubbed her forehead again. "By the way, what's the secret of staying on the back of a horse?"

"A horse!" Becky almost screamed the words. "Don't you dare try and ride a horse again. Are you trying to give your poor mama a heart attack? Listen, sweetie, you don't need to prove you're brave to your mama; your mama knows already." Becky heaved a great sigh. "Law, you're just like your daddy."

"No, I'm not." She should have known better than to mention horses, but Becky had been an accomplished horsewoman in her youth. "I was just wondering, that's all."

"Well, quit it. I won't have my baby getting her poor little face all busted up again." Becky muttered darkly about false friends and added, "And don't you dare go buying yourself a horse. Do you hear me?"

"Yes, Mama." Now she'd done it. She'd be lucky if Becky didn't turn up on her doorstep that evening, determined to prevent Felicity from thinking another thought about horses. "The last thing I have time for right now is a horse."

"Good," Becky said. "How was the barbecue, sweetie? Any eligible bachelors?"

"Come on, Mama. The barbecue was business." Perhaps Becky would forget about horses in favor of casing the eligible bachelors in Foxe.

"You ain't goin' blind, are you, sugar?" Becky asked.

"Mama, I do not attend parties like a buzzard looking for prey," Felicity said. "I'm more like a politician. I leave a business card in each hand I shake."

"You take after your daddy, sweetie," Becky said fondly. "He could have talked a dog off a meat wagon."

"Puh-leeze, Mama." Suspicion struck…Becky was taking the horse matter all too well. "Where are you?"

"Where am I?" She heard sounds, as if Becky was looking about for a road sign. "I'm on my bus and just coming into Huntsville, Alabama, angel. Randy and me are having us a fine old time."

"I knew Randy was in on this," Felicity grumbled.

She hung up the phone thirty minutes later, feeling certain she had distracted Becky's mind from horses.

Her own problem still loomed. In less than twenty hours, she was going to have to mount one of the animals and attempt to ride it while at the same time imitating a super-cool cowgirl who had been born on horseback. Ordinarily, Felicity would have enjoyed the challenge. She just wished this particular one wasn't quite so terrifying.

It was her own fault. She'd let Aaron box her in until she couldn't refuse to ride without looking like a coward. Pride, as Becky was fond of saying, always got a woman kicked in the teeth.

The telephone rang an hour later while Felicity was brewing a cup of nerve-soothing chamomile tea. "Yes, Mama?"

"No horses," Becky said. "Do you hear me?"

"Horses?" Felicity remained wonderfully innocent. "What on earth are you talking about?"

Becky let an ominous silence build then artfully broke the tension as Felicity opened her mouth in another denial. "You're up to something, Felicity Clayton. Don't you think your mama knows?"

"Mama, I am not buying a horse, I promise you."

"I don't want you touching a horse," Becky said. "I don't want you even looking at a horse. If I have to come down there…"

Felicity promised immediately to eschew all horses forever and ever. Pointing out to Becky that she was over twenty-one and had been making her own decisions for years would have been unnecessarily cruel. She had long ago accepted Becky's need to give motherly guidance.

"No horses," Becky repeated, and hung up.

Felicity noted that Becky didn't sound particularly satisfied and mentally kicked herself. She should have known better than to mention horses in the first place. She got out her address book and called each of her five cousins scattered around the state of Tennessee, and chattered about her vacation while she worked the conversation around to horseback riding. The tactic failed five times.

"You know what happened the last time you rode a horse," cousin Jennifer Mills warned. "Forget it, Felicity."

Well, she argued inwardly as she prepared for bed, so what if everyone found out she was a phony whose knees turned to jelly at the sight of a horse? She was selling image, not fact. Nobody really *wanted* to be a cowgirl these days.

But something inside wouldn't let Felicity confess to cowardice and abandon the ride. She'd have to face a horse down one of these days. It might as well be tomorrow, when she had Aaron present to provide the necessary grit.

Felicity climbed into the lumpy bed, chuckling in spite of her fears. With Aaron's contempt to spur her on, she might ride like Annie Oakley.

• • •

"I knew you wouldn't disappoint us," Aaron drawled. He stared appreciatively at Felicity's riding outfit. "It's a good thing we polished up the horses." He looked down at his own dusty jeans and wrinkled, blue work shirt. "Too bad I didn't have time to polish myself."

He stood outside the stables behind his house where two horses and two ponies had been tied to a wooden fence rail. The wide graveled drive leading to the building was bounded by a white, wood-rail fence and dotted with pecan trees. The stable looked even more imposing in the daylight than it had the night before.

Felicity wasn't in the mood to notice the pastoral beauty of her surroundings. Not even concentrating on Aaron's broad shoulders and long, strong legs blocked the object of her anxiety from the forefront of her mind.

The dreaded object twitched a muscle on his flanks and stamped his rear foot. The hollow clomp of Rhyolite's hoof on the graveled walkway resounded through Felicity's mind and body like cymbals clashing.

She came to a dead halt. Rhyolite lifted his head and snorted at her. Felicity's knees turned to rubber. Her heart quaked within her chest. But her face wore the smile a top saleswoman always wore in the face of migraine headaches, hostile prospects, and runners in her stockings.

"Are you sure those jeans were made for riding?" Aaron asked.

Felicity ignored him in favor of concentrating on deep breathing. She had worn a blue cotton shirt trimmed with red and a pair of red jeans so tight she had trouble zipping them up. When she looked at the height of the stirrup she was supposed to place her foot into, she knew the jeans—meant to help hold her erect—had been a major mistake.

Rhyolite tossed his head and stamped his hooves again. She looked down at those hooves. They were the biggest horse hooves she'd ever seen. Stark terror arose in her throat.

"Felicity, look at Donatello," Pete said. "I brushed him myself."

"Felicity, look at Michelangelo," Joey cried.

Felicity turned aside to look. She admired the two well-brushed ponies. Cautiously stroking Donatello's soft muzzle temporarily distracted her quivering nerves.

Beside Rhyolite, a second horse just as big stood quietly. As Felicity's frozen gaze rested on the other horse, he twitched his tail and stamped a foot.

She was going to die this afternoon. She knew it.

Pete patted Donatello's neck. "Let's go, Felicity. This is going to be fun."

Felicity got a grip on herself. She could do it. She could do anything. There was no reason to suppose disaster loomed just because she was about to mount a horse.

She approached Rhyolite cautiously. Her palms were so wet, she probably wouldn't be able to hold the reins. Wiping them on her jeans, she eyed Rhyolite. The big horse stood calmly, swishing his tail gently and ignoring her.

The first big challenge was to get aboard the monster. Felicity swallowed.

"Well, Miss Clayton? Would you like a hand up?"

Startled, she looked at Aaron. He was standing on the other side of the horse watching her expectantly. As if he knew she was going to be stomped, kicked, bitten, or thrown, she thought with considerable indignation.

Felicity's fighting spirit rallied. "No, thank you. I prefer to mount on my own."

The words sounded fine—almost as if she knew what she was talking about. Heartened, she took another step toward Rhyolite while her adrenalin surged and her courage was up. Within about three feet of the big gray gelding, all systems collapsed. Rhyolite tossed his head and looked at her. Felicity halted in her tracks.

Fortunately, the two boys were occupied with untying their ponies' reins. Aaron was leading his horse away from the fence and appeared to be watching the horse's gait.

Now. She had to do it now, while no one was observing. Once in the saddle, she'd cling like a spider monkey until the ordeal ended. But first, she had to get in the saddle.

Felicity dried her damp palms on her hips and searched out the stirrup. How she was supposed to get her boot into a waist-high stirrup, she didn't know. Taking a deep breath, she went for it.

The stirrup felt cold and heavy to her inexperienced hand. Holding it steady, she lifted her foot—a difficult task in her skin-tight jeans—and aimed it at the stirrup.

Rhyolite jerked his head up. His hindquarters made a semicircular motion, and the stirrup fell from Felicity's cold fingers. Every muscle in his enormous body twitched; he snorted and tried to look around at her. It was almost as if the big horse was annoyed with her.

Numb with fear, she approached again. She tried to imagine she was climbing a tree or a fence, some inanimate object that didn't sidle away every time she lifted her foot and tried to place it into the stirrup. Rhyolite couldn't move very far tied to the fence rail, but any movement at all took him out of Felicity's range. Every time she tried to insert her boot into the stirrup, the horse moved.

Felicity forgot her fear in favor of frustration with Rhyolite. Not that she considered this Rhyolite's fault. No, sir. If she didn't know any better, she'd swear Aaron had told the horse to make her look bad. Naturally, Rhyolite had to obey or risk having his oat supply cut off.

She wasn't letting Aaron get away with this. Circling, Felicity came at the horse from a different angle, all too conscious of Aaron watching her as he walked his own horse in a circle.

"Let me give you a leg up." He tied his horse to the fence and took up a position on the gelding's left side. "Looks like Rhyolite is a little testy this morning."

Felicity remained on the right side of the gray gelding. "As you say, he's a very spirited horse."

"You have to get on the other side of Rhyolite, Felicity." Joey had already mounted his pony and was holding the reins like a true cowboy. "He won't let you get on him on that side."

Felicity viewed the horse with hostility. "Is that so?"

"Isn't that right, Uncle Aaron?"

Aaron's smile was a masterpiece of innocence. "That's right, Joey."

Felicity gathered she had just broken a major law of horseback riding, and that Aaron knew it. She hadn't gotten any good advice from her cousins since they knew the disaster that had befallen her on her last great ride. She also hadn't located a book on the subject, since she'd spent the day house cleaning and waiting for various repair persons.

The only thing she could do was bluff.

She sauntered around to where Aaron was waiting to hoist her up. "That's very good, Joey. You really know your stuff. I'm sure your uncle is very proud of you and Pete."

"They're good students," Aaron said.

Felicity gave him a suspicious glance. His smile was so bland, she could have cooked it over water and called it custard.

"I can see they are," she said.

She refused to look at Rhyolite. If she did, she might lose every bit of nerve Aaron's knowing smile gave her. She placed her foot reluctantly in his locked hands and felt her body rise impossibly high in the air.

"Now throw your leg across," Aaron commanded. "Not that one. The other leg. That's it. You're on."

Felicity balanced numbly on the saddle. She was mounted, for what that was worth, but she didn't think she'd be there for long. This was even worse than the last time she'd attempted riding a horse. Rhyolite was so big, she felt like a marble balanced on a two-by-four. Any minute now, she'd roll right off.

"Here are the reins." Aaron passed her the two thin strips of leather that were supposed to control the behemoth. "Don't start without us. I've got a path picked out that's easy and unobstructed."

She clutched the reins so tightly, poor Rhyolite turned in a circle in an effort to obey whatever strange command she was giving him. Felicity gasped and dug in her knees in a vain effort to cling harder. Rhyolite's forelegs rose off the ground in a half-rear. He danced back then shot forward a few steps. Felicity almost somersaulted off; she dragged back so hard on the reins.

"My," she gasped, when the great horse halted. Her teeth chattered with terror. "He sure is spirited."

"Quit tugging the reins," Aaron shouted. "He doesn't know what you want him to do."

With Aaron's sharp navy eyes on her, Felicity hastily put on her professional smile and assumed a relaxed posture.

"You forgot to put your feet in the stirrups," Pete observed. "Isn't she supposed to put her feet in the stirrups, Uncle Aaron?"

"I—uh—used to ride Indian style," Felicity said. "I'm not used to stirrups."

Conscious of Aaron's stare of disbelief, Felicity bent over to look for the stirrups. When she did, she almost slid sideways off the horse. She located them at last, one on each side, and carefully thrust her booted feet into them as tightly as she could manage. They might help hold her in place.

Aaron picked up his horse's left foreleg and examined the hoof. "Corsair has picked up a stone. I thought something was wrong with his gait." He looked up at Felicity. "Would you be very disappointed if I asked you to ride Quiche this afternoon? She isn't quite up to my weight, and I don't have another saddle horse available, so I'll need Rhyolite."

Felicity was ready to faint with relief, even though she strongly suspected Aaron was trying to find a face-saving way to get her off the big horse and onto a smaller, gentler mount.

"I'd be happy to," she said graciously. "I can always ride this wonderful horse another time."

Not if she could help it. Felicity loosened her death grip on the reins and prepared to draw her feet from the stirrups. Unfortunately, she had thrust her boots in so deeply, they wouldn't slide out.

"Hold it," Aaron called. "I'll help you get down."

Felicity didn't think she could sit there knowing Rhyolite—a veritable mountain of muscle and sinew—was beneath her another minute. She jerked back with her heels. The stirrups released their grip and Felicity's heels banged solidly into Rhyolite's flanks.

"Felicity, stop!" Aaron yelled.

The big horse gathered himself and she sat on a heaving mountain. The next thing she knew, Rhyolite launched his body forward. She jerked back and dropped the reins in her desperation to grab his mane. She dug in with her knees and clutched Rhyolite for dear life.

Rhyolite took off like a bottle rocket.

She didn't have time to shriek. The wind pushed any sound she made back down her throat. She relived her entire life within a grand total of five seconds.

Rhyolite flew down the driveway, galloping at full tilt toward the road that ran in front of the house. Gravel flew in all directions from beneath his mighty hooves. The only thing Felicity could see was a blur of grass. She bent forward, gasping, and wrapped her arms in a death grip around the horse's neck. She dimly heard Aaron's shouts and the yells of the two little boys. The rumble of Rhyolite's hooves thundered in her ears.

Tires screeched. A horn blared. Rhyolite reared violently and made a two-legged turn. Felicity felt her body become weightless as she parted company with the saddle on Rhyolite's back. She floated across space and made a three-point landing on Aaron's well-maintained lawn.

She lay on her back, gazing up at the white-blue sky of deep summer. Dazed, Felicity found herself fascinated by a fluffy white cloud hovering overhead. She studied it, dimly amazed that it was so white and so scalloped around the edges. She had never seen a cloud quite like it before.

People bent over her, blocking her view of the sky. It irritated her, but she couldn't summon interest in telling them to move. She focused on the pieces of blue she could see while the summery odor of green grass caressed her senses.

"Felicity, are you all right?" Pete cried. "You really are a good cowgirl. You made old Rhyolite do a pirouette."

Felicity smiled. She didn't know what that meant, but she could see that in Pete's eyes she had earned her cowgirl's spurs.

"Felicity, please get up," Joey pleaded.

"She almost rode that horse over my truck," an aggrieved voice said. "Damn it, Aaron, you ought to be more careful who you let ride that crazy gelding of yours."

"Shut up, Chance." Aaron sounded frantic. "You nearly hit one of my cows last week doing ninety miles an hour down this road. This wouldn't have happened if you'd been driving at a decent speed."

"Felicity," Joey called. "Felicity, wake up."

Felicity was dimly aware of the way Aaron checked her limp body over, tight-lipped and pale with anxiety. Although she found his concern heart-warming, it was misplaced. She felt wonderful.

"Aaron, is she all right?" Deborah approached at a run. "Should I call an ambulance?"

Felicity noted Aaron's concern. But when he tapped her cheek gently with his forefinger, she saw the motion but didn't feel it.

"I don't know," he bit out. "She seems conscious, but I can't get her to respond."

"Felicity, wake up," Pete called.

Felicity wished everyone would quiet down and let her continue her peaceful communing with the summer sky. A full five minutes passed before Felicity's senses fully returned; she wished they hadn't. Everything had been so quiet and restful.

"I think I'm all right," she said at long last. "I just had the breath knocked out of me for a minute."

Aaron sucked in his own breath and carefully lifted her to a sitting position. The moment she sat up unaided, he laid into her.

"You ought to be horse-whipped," he roared. "You nearly got my horse killed."

"Hush, Aaron," Deborah begged. "What if she has a concussion?"

"Your crazy horse nearly dumped me on the road in front of that man's truck," Felicity returned. "I ought to sue you for possessing a wild, unruly animal and making people ride it."

Aaron's mouth opened, but for a moment no sound came out. Then he appeared to find his voice.

"I ought to sue you for pretending you knew how to ride a horse, you phony cowgirl," he shouted. "You've never ridden a horse before in your life, have you? Well? Have you?"

"Aaron, please," Deborah said. "She might be hurt."

"Don't mind him, Deborah," Felicity said. "He's just behaving like a jerk because he's so relieved his stupid horse didn't kill me." She smiled at the driver of the truck. He was a black man in his mid-fifties, short and wiry. "I'm terribly sorry that wild horse of Mr. Whitaker's spooked your truck. If you had ended up in the ditch, it would have been all his fault."

The man looked from her to Aaron with a startled expression on his dark face, then his lips parted in a huge grin. "I'm Chance Breaux, ma'am. Pleased to meet you, I'm sure. You rode that wild horse like a real pro."

Felicity thought it was a shame everyone, no names mentioned, couldn't be as sensible and as decent as Chance Breaux.

"We'd better get her home," Aaron said, frowning.

"Sure thing, Aaron," Chance said, still grinning. "I'll help you. Then I've got to call my lawyer about the suit I'm going to file on you for letting your wild horse scare the life out of my poor little truck."

"If you want to give a lawyer your money, why don't you just mail him a fat donation?" Aaron responded. "He'd be very grateful, and I wouldn't have to speak to Sheriff Darby about the way you race that miserable truck of yours up and down the road in front of my house."

"I'll testify that truck was doing less than twenty-five," Felicity said. "Too bad I didn't break a leg or something. Just think of the huge settlement I'd get."

Aaron straightened and glared down at her. "You're lucky you weren't killed," he rumbled. "Hell, so am I. What a chance for all your greedy relatives to descend. They'd probably clean me out like a freezer full of Blue Bell vanilla ice cream."

"They still might," a vibrant female voice said from behind him.

"Oh, no," Felicity whispered. "*Mama*."

"I just knew something was goin' on around here with horses," Becky Lozano said, brown eyes flashing with outrage. "I just knew it."

Aaron turned. It was obvious he recognized Becky at once.

"And just what have you been doin' to my baby, you low-down rat snake, you?" Becky demanded, hands on hips. "I ain't gonna just clean you out like an ice cream freezer. I'm gonna *skin* you, and then I'm gonna hang that nasty-tempered hide of yours out to dry."

Chapter 5

Aaron stood quietly to one side and tried not to call attention to himself. It wasn't easy in Lureen Tucker's tiny, junk-filled living room.

"You can quit being mean to him now, Mama," Felicity said from her reclining position on the sofa. "He's let you order him around like a slave for the last ten minutes, so let him go home, please."

Becky ignored her daughter and ignored Aaron, who stood ready to offer any help Becky might need. It was, he figured, the least he could do after what had almost happened to Becky's daughter.

"Law, that woman was the meanest old witch that ever lived," Becky said, disgusted. "Just look at this mess."

"You're lucky I've cleaned off the sofa," Felicity said. "But it's going to take a lot more time than I thought to go through everything. You should have waited another two weeks, Mama."

"I want you getting rid of all this nasty, moldy old furniture. Ain't nobody gonna want it. You, there." Becky stood in the center of the living room, alternately glaring at the room and at Aaron. "Go fetch my baby an ice pack for her poor little forehead. And while you're at it, make her a cup of that chamomile tea."

"My head is fine, Mama. Let Mr. Whitaker go home."

Becky sped Aaron on his way to the kitchen with a ferocious gesture. "He ain't leaving this house until I'm sure my baby is all right. I knew something terrible was going to happen to you when you came down here to this place. I just knew it. That old witch cursed everything she ever touched."

"Now, Mama, it's time to let bygones be bygones."

"Nothing doing," Becky said. "I ought to go spit on her grave."

"Now, Mama—" Felicity began.

"Don't you 'now, Mama' me, Felicity Clayton. How dare that ungrateful old biddy go around sayin' you robbed her bank account?" Becky took a furious turn around the room. "I told you what would happen if you extended a helpin' hand to her, so don't say I didn't warn you. She may have been my mother, but she was a wicked, vicious old hag. It's her fault you're lyin' there at death's door this very minute."

Aaron stood quietly in the kitchen, just out of sight, and listened, unabashed. Like almost everyone who enjoyed country music, he was familiar with the high points of Becky Lozano's career. But he never had a clue that Lureen Tucker was Becky's mother. No one had. It was incredible.

"I'm hardly at death's door." Felicity's voice was deliberately pitched, he suspected, to soothe her mother. "She was mentally sick. You can't hold anything against her."

"Oh, yes, I can," Becky spat. "I could've forgiven her for anything she ever did to me—and that was a lot, let me tell you— but *never* for what she did to my baby."

Felicity abandoned that argument. "Well, she certainly didn't have anything to do with me trying to ride that horse."

Fascinated, Aaron took care not to advertise his presence in the kitchen by rattling or clinking anything.

"Don't you try and tell me she didn't cause this," Becky snarled. "Fenton told me what she was tellin' people."

"Mama..."

"And I'll bet all the neighbors around here think you stole your own money from the old witch. You in there," Becky called. "Where's that ice pack?"

Aaron appeared with ice in a plastic bag and a clean dish towel. He hoped his expression conveyed his deep concern for Felicity's health. She lay with her eyes closed while Becky lovingly tended to her forehead. Aaron had never seen anything like it.

At least, not since the time two weeks ago when he'd watched Deborah place a similar pack on Joey when he fell and bumped his forehead. It was clear Becky intended to nurse her daughter back to health as if Felicity was a child.

Felicity lay in silence while Becky ordered Aaron back to the kitchen. When he returned with the chamomile tea, Becky carefully centered the tea cup on the coffee table within easy reach of Felicity's hand.

Aaron said nothing. He knew better than to speak until Becky gave him leave. He'd thoughtfully made Becky a cup of chamomile tea also, and he set it on the coffee table before her.

After carrying Felicity in his arms all the way across his lawn and Felicity's to the accompaniment of Becky's scolding, he had offered further assistance. It looked as though Becky intended to make full use of his services.

Felicity's brown eyes, so similar to Becky's, watched him warily from beneath the edge of the ice pack. Aaron felt so ashamed of himself, he could hardly meet Felicity's gaze. He still couldn't believe he had been so obtuse. He had taken Lureen's rambling statements as fact, even though he'd known she wasn't quite normal.

It served him right if he had to grovel a little. He stared at Felicity's slender figure and swallowed. He couldn't have lived with himself if she'd been seriously hurt.

Becky gulped down scalding chamomile tea. "Thanks. I ain't usually so rude, but seeing my baby all laid out on the ground by that awful bronco of yours was just too much."

"My apologies, Ms. Lozano." Aaron made no foolish attempt to defend his horse. "I should never have let her ride Rhyolite."

"You sure as heck shouldn't have," Becky agreed, although her rich voice sounded much more mellow.

"She's a very brave young woman," Aaron said. "Not just anyone could stay on Rhyolite the way she did."

Felicity rolled her eyes. He could see the slight movements of her face beneath the ice pack before Becky reached over and adjusted it.

Becky collapsed onto one of the dirty old armchairs that Felicity had thrown a sheet over. "Law, that child reminds me of her daddy more and more every day. Tell her she can't do somethin', and that's exactly what she goes and does. What's a poor mother to do?"

Aaron glanced at Felicity. She looked like a fallen cowgirl—a very colorful fallen cowgirl. He wanted to hold her and comfort away the residual terror he was sure she still felt, but the brown eyes glinting from under the ice pack warned him against that action.

"She has the sweetest little apartment in Nashville," Becky said. "All my relatives help look after her. So maybe you can tell me what possessed her to come down here to this awful place instead of taking a nice Caribbean cruise or something if she wanted a vacation." She shot another disgusted glance at the piles of old political magazines and newspapers that littered most of the floor space.

"A desire for independence?" Aaron asked, his voice a soft rumble.

He was pushing it, he knew, but he couldn't stop himself. There was a lot more to Felicity Clayton than her fancy cowgirl clothes and he wanted to know more about her.

"Independence." Becky reared up to frown at him. "She's way too independent as it is. I sent her off to college so she wouldn't grow up to be ignorant like I am, and what did she do? She decided she wanted to be a saleswoman. A *saleswoman*. And she took off all by herself through the whole state of Tennessee sellin' *tractors*."

"That's tough on a mother," Aaron said. He could imagine young farmers all over Tennessee lining up to buy tractors from Felicity.

"No one can possibly call you ignorant, Mama," Felicity said. "Your manager says you're the smartest businesswoman he's ever dealt with."

"I didn't say I wasn't smart," Becky countered. "I said I was ignorant 'cause I quit school in the ninth grade. Your daddy wanted you to grow up and maybe be a teacher or something. We didn't raise you to be no saleswoman." Becky sipped tea, much aggrieved and looked at the ceiling. "Sorry, Johnny. I did my best, but she won't listen to me."

"She's selling clothes now?" Aaron stared at Felicity.

Becky gave a short laugh. "Yep. Cowgirl clothes. Ain't that a hoot? I thought she'd settle down when she turned twenty-one and inherited the money her daddy left her, but no, that wasn't what she did. She bought my crazy old mama this house to keep her far away and out of my hair and then she took a job sellin' heavy equipment all over the southern United States. After she almost turned me into a nervous wreck, she bought a shop in Nashville and moved home. At last."

Becky was on a roll, Aaron realized, and nothing was going to stop her until she'd released all the nervous tension she'd built up from worrying over her daughter.

He tried to remember Becky Lozano's history, or the version that had been given to the media. "I thought her father died when she was a baby."

"He did." Becky sighed and sipped tea. "But he stays around helpin' me get her raised." She lifted her tea cup to the ceiling in a salute to an unseen presence. "Guess he knows she takes after him too much and wants to help. How's your head, baby?"

Aaron didn't miss the tender, cooing note that entered Becky's voice when she spoke to Felicity. He also noted the dry, laughter-tinged tone in which Felicity replied. Felicity understood and indulged her mother's need to care for her. Aaron had never seen anything like it.

"It's much better, Mama. May I take the ice pack off?"

Becky studied her watch. "Let's leave it on a few more minutes, baby. We don't want anything bruised now, do we?"

"No, Mama. Let Mr. Whitaker go on home. He's got a lot of things to see to this afternoon."

Aaron knew Felicity wanted to get him out of the house, but he wasn't about to leave. "I'd better stick around a little longer, Ms. Lozano. Just in case your daughter turns out to have a concussion."

Becky turned toward the sofa, alarmed.

"Not that she does," he hastened to add. "I think she's only shaken up. Felicity, would you mind telling me why you pretended you were an experienced rider?"

"I am an experienced rider," Felicity snapped, glaring at him with one unobstructed brown eye.

"What?" Becky sat up, astounded. "She ain't no more an experienced rider than a baby."

"An experienced rider is someone who has ridden a horse before," Felicity hastened to point out. "I've ridden a horse before."

"Bull." Becky sprang to her feet. "You spent more time flyin' through the air than you did on the horse's back. And your poor little mouth. I nearly fainted when I first saw you layin' there on that hospital bed."

Aaron studied Felicity's mouth, appalled. "What happened to her mouth?"

"Why, she busted up every tooth in her head." Becky waved her hands. The trauma of the event was obviously still fresh in her mind. "Even her poor little jaw was all shattered. They put everything back together again, thank God, but that's why she's still wearin' all that metal stuff on her teeth. Gotta wear it another year, the doctor says."

Aaron thought back, shocked. The album Becky released almost a year ago contained several songs about a loved one in the hospital. No one could get more pathos out of an event than

Becky Lozano. Now that he'd met her, Aaron realized Becky felt ordinary things the way all great artists did, with tremendous depth and verve.

"Come on, Mama," Felicity said. "It wasn't that bad. The damage was mostly cosmetic, except for the injury to my pride. Let Mr. Whitaker go on home."

"How badly were you hurt?" Aaron asked.

He stared at Felicity, stunned. He would never, never have let her get anywhere near a horse if he'd known that. She must have been terrified, but she had managed to cover it so well, he hadn't realized there was a serious problem until she was already mounted on Rhyolite. Then, when it was too late, he'd finally put the correct interpretation on the way she'd reacted in the stable yesterday.

He had suspected she was bluffing about her riding ability, but he hadn't realized she had any reason to fear horses.

"Mama's exaggerating." Felicity's full lips tightened. "I was only in the hospital a few hours while a dental surgeon looked me over."

"You could've been killed," Becky said. "The yellow-bellied little weasel responsible had better not *ever* show his face in Nashville again."

"Mama sued him," Felicity said, carefully expressionless. "At least, the suit will be processed if they can ever find him."

"Danged right, I sued him." Becky's powerful voice rose a notch. "Hurtin' my baby like that."

"Lord knows what she'll do to *you*." Felicity regarded Aaron with considerable relish. "Maybe you'd better move to another planet while you still can."

Aaron stared, entranced. Here was a woman who knew how to enjoy being protected without allowing herself to be dominated. No wonder she had seen straight through his tough-guy act.

"Now, baby," Becky said. "The poor man is sorry as can be. I always admire a man who stays and faces the music instead of turnin' tail like that coward of a Gary Carlisle you were so sweet on. Besides, it's perfectly clear to me that you had some kinda silly idea in your head about provin' you could ride a horse."

"Guess I'll have to sue you myself," Felicity muttered, miming disappointment.

Aaron grinned appreciatively and marked the name of Gary Carlisle for future reference.

Now that he saw the two women together, there was no doubt Felicity was Becky's daughter. They both had slender faces with identical large brown eyes, although Becky's wiry brown hair had been bleached and hennaed into a spectacular red-gold color. Aaron decided he preferred Felicity's natural color.

He looked again at Felicity. Even lying on the sofa with an ice pack on her forehead, she drew his attention. What really got him was that he'd hardly even looked at a woman in the past unless she was a blue-eyed blonde who hung upon his every word.

He was definitely in trouble. If he had any sense, he'd bow out now and leave Becky Lozano in charge of her daughter's recovery. He didn't need this impossible attraction on top of everything else going on in his life.

"Law." Becky leaned back and swigged more chamomile tea. "What a day. I just knew she was hiding somethin' from her mama, so I told my manager, I said, Chester, I've got to go see about my baby. And he was understandin' about it. He really, really was." She gulped more tea then set the empty cup aside. "But I ain't gonna make it back to Dallas tonight. My baby's health is more important."

Felicity shoved herself up. The ice pack slid off her forehead. "Mama, you're not going to stay here if you're supposed to be doing a concert in Dallas. I'm perfectly fine. Just a trifle shaken up, that's all."

Becky leaped up and replaced the ice pack. She pressed Felicity back down on the sofa. "I'm the mama around here, and I say I ain't goin' nowhere while my baby needs me."

"Mama, I'm all right."

"Don't you lie to me, Felicity Clayton. I'm stayin' right here until I'm sure you ain't had no concussion like you did last time." She sat down on the edge of the sofa and stroked Felicity's cheek. "I know you want to be up and doin', and when I look at this place, I can see why. That crazy old woman turned it into a regular pigsty. I told you she would."

"When I get through with this house, it'll be a model country cottage."

"Law." Becky cast a doubtful look around. "I guess writin' nasty letters to the president of the United States and all the congressmen didn't leave her much time for cleanin' house."

Aaron had to admit that this summed up Lureen Tucker's life quite succinctly. He might as well find out the rest of what had puzzled him for the past few years.

"Who is Fenton Mills?" he asked.

Becky looked at him in her straightforward way. "Fenton is my mother's brother. My uncle, in other words, but nobody knows that, and we'd both kinda like to keep it that way. Fenton never wanted her to know where he lived, 'cause she probably would've got him fired from his job. She was like that."

"I see." Aaron remembered that Lureen's rambling talk had been filled with righteous statements about her relatives' evil natures.

"My baby here, when she inherited the trust her daddy left for her, she thought that if we bought my mama a house far away from Nashville and gave her money to stay in it, we'd all be a lot happier." Becky rolled her eyes. "And she was right. We were. I could concentrate on my career without worryin' about Mama lyin' to reporters about my personal life." Becky brooded a moment. "She can call me a scarlet woman all she wants, but when she starts attackin' my baby…"

Aaron recalled a great many rambling comments about stages and scarlet women Lureen made, statements so general, he had never connected them with anyone. The remarks about her greedy granddaughter, however, had hit him hard, especially when the flashy, brown-eyed cowgirl had arrived to take possession within a week of Lureen's death.

"Wasn't till my baby bought her this house and put her in it that I was able to develop my career," Becky said.

Aaron knew enough about Becky's history to know this was true. She had been on the fringe of the country scene for almost twenty years. About five years ago, she had literally burst into the forefront, passing up the eager, younger singers with her powerful, gut-wrenching songs.

"'Course it helped when my little girl bought me a bus and helped me hire a first-class band," Becky said, grinning. "Just goes to show you—when you raise your babies right, they don't mind doin' things for you." She laughed her powerful, throaty laugh. "Either that, or they're tryin' to find a nice way to make you quit smotherin' 'em."

Aaron glanced at Felicity, grinning.

Felicity covered her face with the ice pack. "If that's what I was trying to do, it sure didn't work, did it?"

"No, baby," Becky said tenderly. "You're just too soft-hearted to get tough and tell your mama to butt out."

The telephone rang. Becky shoved herself out of the sheet-covered chair and picked up her empty cup. "Drink that tea, baby. And keep that ice pack on your head."

The moment Becky left the room, Felicity sat up and removed the ice pack. She reached for the tea sitting beside her and gulped half the cup before she faced Aaron.

"You'd better go now, before Mama comes back," she said, replacing the tea cup with trembling hands.

"I'd better stick around," Aaron said. "If I'm not here to defend myself, she might change her mind about suing me."

"Look, if you'll go now, I promise I won't let her sue you. She's got to get to Dallas and do that show."

He put on a thoughtful expression. "I can help—"

"Felicity Clayton, you get back on that couch," Becky bellowed from the kitchen. She stood as close to the door as the telephone cord allowed. "Now, you listen to me, Chester. My baby needs me, and you're just goin' to have to explain that to the folks. They'll understand. They know how I feel about my baby."

Felicity struggled to rise to a standing position.

Aaron came to her side instantly and lifted her to her feet, then kept a supportive hand beneath her elbow.

"Look, Mama, I'm fine. I want you getting back on that highway right now so you can sing tonight for the fans."

"I ain't goin'." Becky covered the receiver with one hand and regarded Felicity with concern. "You don't look so good, baby."

"I'm fine, Mama. Really. That ice pack of yours froze all the color out of my face."

While Felicity argued with her mother, Aaron concentrated on her. She was still pale and shaky, which worried him to no end. Maybe he ought to drive her to the community hospital for a thorough check-over.

On the other hand, there was nothing wrong with her brain or her tongue. Once more, Aaron cursed himself for being so totally blind to her fear of horses. Ordinarily, he detected nuances of people's behavior, but he had been so annoyed with Felicity and the situation in general that he had ignored any signs.

Resolving to think about that later, Aaron considered how best to help Felicity now. It was obvious Felicity cared as much about her mother's career as Becky did and wasn't about to let Becky disappoint her fans.

"You don't have to worry about a thing, Ms. Lozano," Aaron said. "My sister and I will be more than happy to lend your daughter our guest room for the night. I'll keep an eye on her personally."

Becky looked at him, and Aaron returned her stare. He had the feeling that Becky's gaze had turned into a powerful scanning microscope trained on his very soul.

"That's mighty thoughtful of you, Mr. Whitaker," Becky said slowly.

"Call me Aaron." He noticed that her thick, Kentucky-mountain accent had become much less noticeable, and a smile twitched his mouth.

Becky uncovered the telephone receiver, her gaze fixed on Aaron's mouth, and said, "Chester, I'll be there. Just stand by till I tell you what airfield I'm comin' in on." She hung up. "Maybe you'd better call me Becky. You're interested in my accent."

"Your accent is charming," Aaron said. "My problem was that I couldn't quite figure out which part of the country you hailed from."

Becky threw her head back and laughed. "That's because I use a little bit of everything. I was born in Hoover, Kentucky, and I've played every honky-tonk in the South. This voice came from Kentucky, Tennessee, Texas, and Alabama, with a little bit of Cajun tossed in for spice. Law, I'm glad I met you. I ain't told anybody that in years."

"Why tell him?" Felicity muttered. "He might sell the story to some tabloid tomorrow."

"Now, baby, he don't need none of my money," Becky said soothingly. Her sharp, brown gaze scanned her daughter knowingly. "Besides, the way I've been talkin' half out of my head today, he's got a lot more than that he could tell a tabloid if he wanted to. Ain't none of 'em ever got hold of the true story about my mama."

"That's because everybody has a crazy relative or two," Felicity said. "Let's call the airport. If you're going to make Dallas in time for your concert tonight, you'll have to leave shortly."

Becky jerked on the phone cord, disgusted. "Law, I thought nobody had an ol' dialin' phone like this anymore. Where's the phone book? I'll bet she used the pages from it to light the stove the way she used to when I was a kid."

"I picked one up at the Chamber of Commerce yesterday, Mama." Felicity presented the book.

"That li'l ol' thing is a phone book?"

"It's a growing city, Mama."

"Law." Becky riffled through the pages. "Are you sure there's enough people around here so you can sell this house?"

"There's a new chemical plant going up nearby. Somebody will buy it."

Becky muttered, but she found a number and dialed. "Let's hope so. I'd hate for you to lose all the money you spent on this place, just to help out your poor mama."

"Not to worry, Mama." Felicity pulled out one of the rickety kitchen chairs and sat down. "I'll bet I can sell enough cowgirl outfits to the ladies around here to make up the difference."

Aaron had seen salespeople like Felicity before. They never worried about losing their jobs. They simply went out and got another one, secure in their own ability to sell.

He tested one of the chairs and decided against it. Lureen left those chairs outside to hold her screwball political posters for weeks on end. The weather had not been kind to them.

Becky booked a flight to Dallas and replaced the telephone regretfully. "I'll have to leave in an hour, but before I do, let's have a look around for those songs of mine. I don't suppose you've turned up any sign of them?" She looked hopefully at Felicity.

"No, but it's early days yet. I told you, I'm going to sort through every single piece of paper in the place. If they're here, I'll find them."

"You're looking for some songs you wrote?" Aaron asked, astonished.

So that was why Felicity had come here. Chagrin heated his face.

"Law, yes," Becky said, shaking her head. "I—" She broke off, breathing hard. Her fists clenched. "Johnny—my husband, Johnny Clayton—was the first person ever to believe in me. We were so much in love, and I was pregnant with our baby. Those songs were the best work I've ever done in my life. They were written 'specially for him and for my baby." Two big tears rolled down her cheeks. "That crazy old woman stole them because she couldn't stand that I was happy."

"Now, Mama, don't think about it," Felicity said. "If she hid them here in this house, I'll find them. The minute I do, I'll call you."

Aaron realized the two women were best friends besides being mother and daughter. Becky would kill to protect her baby, and it was obvious enough that Felicity, in spite of her understandable desire for independence, was Becky's chief comfort and supporter.

Becky collapsed into one of the chairs, which wobbled alarmingly, and put her face in her hands. "I'll never forgive her for that. Never. Johnny got killed, and my whole world just collapsed." More tears rolled down her cheeks. "I could never recreate those songs unless I could *feel* them again. They're lost forever."

"Mama, they're here somewhere." Felicity rushed to hug her mother. "You know what a packrat she was. Now, don't worry anymore. I'll find them."

Becky turned into her daughter's embrace. "I know you'll try, baby. But all the same—Hey!" The chair collapsed. Since Becky's arms were around Felicity's neck, Felicity tumbled to the floor with her.

Felicity sat up, laughing, and watched Aaron gently lift Becky to her feet. Then he reached for her. Felicity looked away, flushing slightly, and pretended not to see his hand while she struggled to rise on her own.

Becky brushed off her form-fitting jeans. "Law, this ol' furniture has got to go. Well, Aaron, you'd better help my little girl up while I go pack her a night case. Sure makes me feel better, knowing you're next door here to look out for her." She smiled blandly at her red-faced daughter. "This sure ain't Nashville, baby, but I guess it'll do for a while."

Chapter 6

Felicity dragged her brown hair into a thick ponytail. She wore an ancient t-shirt and a pair of shorts in preparation for a day of major housecleaning, but she was so stiff, she could hardly bend over. She crept into the crowded living room and reached for the shade covering the window facing the Whitaker spread. The shade flew out of her hand and rolled up with a loud rattle, and a blast of bright sunlight struck her eyes.

She studied Aaron's smooth, manicured lawn with jealousy and tried to feel happy not to catch a glimpse of him. After all, she had managed to shut the door on him the day before, the minute Becky's rented car had disappeared down the road. Not even an indignant telephone call from Becky later that night could coerce her to spend the night at his house.

To his credit, Aaron had accepted her decision with good grace and sent his sister, accompanied by his two chocolate Labrador retrievers, over with a tray of hot food. Felicity had lacked the heart to refuse the food.

"Are you sure you won't spend the night with us?" Deborah had asked. "Aaron is on the phone right now with your mother. She's very concerned."

"Mama and your brother are two of a kind," Felicity said. "Let them commiserate with each other." She admired the two beautiful dogs, called Max and Coye, and reflected that she hadn't been too terribly far off when she thought Aaron might have lost a matched pair of fine canines.

Deborah regarded her with awe. "I wish I was as brave as you are. I'd be terrified in this house alone."

"It's not so bad, now that I've had a locksmith out to fix the locks. And when I get all the magazines and junk paper cleared out, it won't be a fire hazard any longer."

"You must be used to living alone," Deborah observed. "I'd be up all night, listening to the house creaking."

"Or the cockroaches walking across the floor. But now that the exterminator has been out, I won't have that problem any longer. And you can tell your brother that the well will be professionally covered tomorrow morning."

"I'll tell him." Deborah smothered a giggle. "I thought he was going to pass out when he turned around and saw your mother."

They had laughed together over the image of Aaron towering over an enraged Becky Lozano and meekly accepting her scolding. Then Deborah and the two labs returned home, leaving Felicity alone.

The hot, delicious rice casserole had done a lot to assuage her feelings, and she went to bed after a long, soaking bath and slept hard. All too soon, morning sunlight called her forth from the soft, lumpy warmth of the bed.

The telephone rang. Felicity told herself she welcomed the excuse to leave the window and miss a possible glimpse of Aaron leaving his house to go to work.

"What took you so long to answer, sugar?" Becky demanded. "Are you sure you're all right? Maybe I'd better call Aaron."

"Don't you dare," Felicity practically howled. Hearing her mother speak Aaron's name in that matter-of-fact way told her Becky thought she had found a surrogate to look after her daughter in her absence. "That man isn't setting foot across my threshold."

Becky was genuinely baffled. "But, why, baby? He's just the sweetest man. Did you know he took care of his little sister like a daddy? And that—?"

"No, Mama," Felicity interrupted. "Furthermore, I don't want to know. Aaron Whitaker and I are two very different people."

Becky was silent. Felicity could almost hear the wheels turning in her mother's brain.

"Law, you're just like your daddy," Becky said at last. "He'd take a downer on someone, and there wasn't nothin' I could say that would change that stubborn mind of his."

Felicity's father had died before she was a year old, but thanks to Becky, Felicity would know him if she met him on the street. "Yes, Mama."

Becky went silent again, a state so uncommon it made Felicity nervous. Becky of all people ought to know why Felicity was wary of men.

"I've got a lot of work to do," Felicity went on. "I've got to clean this house and hunt those songs of yours, plus I've got to go buy a new cell phone sometime today and get this house listed with a realtor. I don't have time to be nice to a man who's caused me nothing but trouble ever since I pulled in the driveway of this house."

"Well, sugar," Becky said, "I have to say, I think you're wrong about Aaron, but far be it from me to bang my head against a brick wall. Now I want you going back to bed, you hear me? Aaron said you'd probably be pretty sore."

"I am not sore," Felicity lied. "The long, soaking bath last night took care of that. But don't worry, Mama. I'll go back to bed if it'll make you feel better."

"It will," Becky said, and hung up.

Felicity returned to the living room, where she methodically moved several stacks of periodicals to the couch. Every magazine and every newspaper had to be searched for Becky's lost songs. Cleaning the house would be a long, tedious process.

Someone knocked at the front door. Felicity figured she'd know that knock anywhere. She ignored both the knock and the corresponding leap of her heart.

"Felicity?" Aaron called. "Are you all right?"

"I'm just fine," she called back. "I'm very busy right now." She settled on the sofa and bent over a magazine. Not for anything was she letting him inside.

"Open up," he said. "I want to talk to you."

"Well, I don't want to talk to you. Will you please go away and leave me alone?"

"Look, I'd like to apologize. I can't apologize to the door."

"Why not?"

The truth was, she figured she had nothing to forgive him for, but God forbid he find that out. Worse, she had the uncomfortable feeling that if she opened the door, she'd melt beneath his potent charm. Aaron was dangerous to her peace of mind. Her best bet was to keep him on the other side of the door.

Aaron remained silent a moment. "Look, I don't blame you for thinking I'm the world's worst jackass, but—"

"You said it," Felicity said, with relish.

"—I thought I had reason."

"Hah. If you run that car dealership of yours on that kind of hearsay, you'll be bankrupt in six months."

She figured his silence meant he was debating just opening the door and walking in. Thank goodness the lock worked now.

"The least you could do is open the door and face me," he said coaxingly.

"Not today, thank you," Felicity called back. "I've already faced down three big roaches this morning. I don't need any confrontations with rats."

"Your mother wants me to look you over. For some reason, she doesn't trust your own assessment of your condition."

"Too bad." Felicity grinned to herself. "Maybe you can convince her that you saw me. It's all a matter of attitude," she added. "Positive thinking and visualization. They'll add the right intonation to your voice—instant believability."

"I'll bet."

She heard his boots click across the creaking wooden porch and clatter down the steps. Only then did she hobble to the window in time to watch as he covered the overgrown grass with long strides. He moved like an athlete.

Felicity sighed then caught herself. Aaron was trouble. A wise woman would get away from that window and put herself back to work.

She waited until he disappeared through his own front door before turning back to the sofa. After all, a woman with sore muscles shouldn't move too fast.

She opened all the windows of the small house to take advantage of the fresh morning air, then finished leafing through the first magazine on the stack and tossed it into the trash sack sitting beside her.

Suddenly, a loud roaring filled her ears. Felicity dropped the next magazine and hurried to the door as fast as her complaining body would allow. The lawn service she had hired wasn't due until tomorrow.

She opened the door and shouted, "Aaron Whitaker, you stop that! I don't want my yard mowed by you."

He never heard her. Moving in harmony to his own inner rhythm, Aaron guided his tractor across the tall grass, leaving a flat, green path in his wake.

Felicity unlatched the screen and stepped out onto the porch, hands on her hips. "Stop."

He mowed on, turning in a perfect square to start back across the yard. She made her way down the front steps and planted herself where he couldn't help but see her.

Aaron caught sight of her, smiled, waved, and kept on mowing. Felicity yelled again. He waved again and mowed on, deliberately ignoring her angry motions.

Felicity glared after Aaron's back as he turned a corner. Unless she wanted to physically confront him and probably get herself mowed, there was nothing she could do to stop him. She went back inside and locked the door.

Standing behind a curtain, she ignored her own work and watched as her overgrown front yard morphed into a smooth, green carpet. At least, that's what she pretended she was watching. In reality, she was waiting for the moment when Aaron stripped off his blue work shirt and let the sun beat down on his bare back.

There was no doubt about it, Felicity thought. The man ought to be outlawed. He ought to be in jail. He ought to be anywhere other than on her small property. He probably knew exactly what he was doing when he stripped off that shirt. He should be arrested.

Felicity stared, intrigued against her will. She had never realized before how artistic the arrangement of a man's musculature was, or how breathtaking the movement of those muscles as they operated together could be. In fact, she'd never been interested in watching a man without his shirt before. This meant big trouble.

She pulled up a chair. A person contemplating trouble needed to get as comfortable as possible.

She moved her chair from window to window and leafed through magazines while Aaron drove his tractor back and forth across her entire yard, front and back. When he finished and drove the tractor back to his own property, she remained at the window dreaming, only to be jolted from her semi-dozing state a little later by loud pounding.

Felicity leaped off the chair and groaned when every muscle protested the action. She jerked open the front door and realized the noise she heard hadn't come from someone knocking her door down. Aaron knelt at the end of the porch, hammer in hand. While she watched, he took a nail from a leather pouch around his waist and drove it into a loose board.

He now wore a white t-shirt that highlighted his tan and gave her a close-up view of the way the muscles in his shoulders coordinated the motion when he reached for anything. She cleared her throat loudly.

"If you're choking, you'll have to do the Heimlich maneuver on yourself," Aaron said. "This porch is going to keep me busy for quite a while."

"If you aren't a licensed carpenter, you shouldn't be touching those boards," Felicity informed him. "What if I walk across this porch and a board flips up and smacks me in the face? I'll probably become the richest woman in Texas."

"Not if you're already planning on suing me, honey." He pounded in another nail. "Assuming you win, all you'll get is a blue pickup truck and a hundred head of Brahman cattle. The bank owns everything else."

Felicity stepped out on the porch and peered across the road at the peaceful group of humped, red cattle grazing there. "I could use a few cows around here. A cow would probably be good company." She glanced pointedly around her newly mowed yard. "I'll bet a cow would keep the grass down, too. Just think. No more tractors roaring around while I'm trying to sleep." She took a step back when Aaron's sharp gaze went over her. "I could tie a bow around her neck and call her Elsie."

Aaron gave her a slow, hot smile and laid down his hammer. "Are you sure you wouldn't rather have my bull? He's registered and worth a lot more than a cow."

"Well, isn't that just like a man?" Felicity tried to work up some indignation. "Cows are the ones that give the milk and have the calves. Since when is a bull worth more than a cow?"

"Since I paid plenty for this particular bull," Aaron returned, chuckling. He rose to his feet with slow grace. "These cattle are breeding stock. A good Red Brahman bull can produce something like twenty calves a year, while a cow produces only one calf a year."

Felicity gasped with feigned outrage. "The day I see a bull producing even one calf is the day I'll win the Nobel Prize in biology."

"Now, Miss Clayton, let's not split hairs over the mechanics of bovine reproduction. You're just looking for something to fight with me about."

"I knew you were a male chauvinist the minute I saw you. Get off my porch, you sexist Neanderthal."

"Now, honey." He took a step toward her. "Look at it from a rancher's perspective."

"You're not a rancher; you're a car salesman." Pleased that she was still capable of pretending anger at a man whose very movements filled her with a sense of delighted anticipation, she flung out her hand in a dramatic gesture. "Off my porch."

Aaron took another step toward her. "In that case, let's discuss trading that Dodge of yours in on a new Chevy truck."

Somehow she managed to overcome the inclination to back up as he approached. This was a moment to stand her ground. After all, he couldn't very well kiss her on the front porch in full view of anyone driving down the road.

Could he? Her breathing quickened with expectation.

"I like my truck, thank you," she said, on a gasp.

"Miss Clayton, I admire your taste." Aaron halted when he stood about three feet from her. "A lady with such great fashion sense shouldn't waste her good taste on a Dodge."

"A Dodge?" Felicity stared into his navy eyes and was lost... almost. She pulled her thoughts back to reality. "My Dodge is practically brand new."

"A Chevy truck would do a lot more for those fancy cowgirl clothes of yours." He reached out slowly and curled his fingers gently around her upper arms. "Why don't you let me show you around the lot? One of the new double-cabs would be my recommendation for you. Your choice of colors, of course."

"What?" Mesmerized, Felicity stared at his tanned face as he leaned toward her very slowly. His rugged features caught the morning sunlight on every plane.

But all male, Felicity thought dreamily, as Aaron's lips settled gently over hers. It was a positively stunning face, one that projected strength and security. At the same time, the expression in those dark blue eyes promised excitement and challenge. Ordinarily, she relished both. In this case, her innate caution warned her that this man might prove even more dangerous to her peace of mind than she had ever imagined.

She ignored it and leaned into his warm strength. Her arms wrapped around his neck. She felt the answering quiver of his body as he pulled her to him. The next thing she knew, his tongue had slipped between her teeth, and he was exploring her tongue and the inner surfaces of her mouth eagerly.

She decided Aaron felt almost like Rhyolite during the short time she'd sat upon his back; a massive collation of muscle and sinew that spoke of speed and power. But rather than intimidate her, Aaron's vital body made her almost heady with a sense of her own feminine power.

He shook when she drew her fingers through his dark hair and let them feather across his ear. His breath hissed through his teeth when she ran her palms down his back and traced his ribs. All that power, and it was hers to command …

When she began exploring his big body with her hands, he groaned aloud.

"Hey," he whispered, against her soft, springy hair. "If you don't cut that out, I'll throw you down and ravish you right here on this porch."

Felicity stiffened. What was she doing, cavorting with the enemy like this? He didn't want her. He was another would-be country singing star who probably wanted to use her relationship to Becky Lozano to promote his singing career.

Or so she had better convince herself.

Aaron drew back slightly and gave her a tender smile. "Not that ravishing you on the porch isn't something I'd like very much to try."

She blanked out the interesting image his words conjured. "I'll bet. Well, let me tell you something, Mr. Whitaker."

"Since we're going to be friends now, don't you think we ought to be on a first-name basis?"

Friends? She blinked at him. Usually, men tried to get her into bed right away in hopes Becky would hear about it and start looking into musical opportunities for her baby's new boyfriend.

"You're right, honey." Aaron grinned when she stared back at him in disbelief. "I don't want to be just your friend."

"Is that so?" Here was where he should suggest that they adjourn to the bedroom.

"Friends don't exchange kisses as potent as this one."

"What?"

Potent kisses? She was losing it. Felicity squeezed her eyes shut and struggled to think straight.

"In fact, I don't think I've ever kissed anyone before and almost went up in flames," he pursued.

That did it. If she didn't shut him up, she might let herself be seduced by words. She had to admit, Aaron had a much better idea of how to go about getting her into bed than the others who had tried.

She ignored the knowledge that Aaron had given no sign of fawning over Becky, or of even mentioning his one-time efforts as a country singer while Becky was there. Perhaps he was just more clever than the others.

She whisked herself out of his loosened hold and threw up her hand. "Hold it right there, Aaron Whitaker. My mother raised me better than to go around kissing strange men in public, even if it is my own front porch."

"I don't doubt it." He laughed outright. "But I thought that since you've spent your entire life doing exactly as you please in spite of your mother…"

Felicity sputtered. How had she gotten herself into this? More to the point, how would she extricate herself?

"I mean," Aaron said softly, "I thought that since you've successfully evaded every other plan your mother made for your life, why not sit down here on the edge of the porch and kiss me again?"

Felicity managed an affronted sniff, but it sounded forced even to her own ears. "I don't want to kiss anyone, thank you very much. I'm a busy woman."

"You could make time to kiss me if you wanted to," Aaron coaxed. He put out both hands, slow and easy, and framed her face lightly with his fingertips, barely touching her soft, vital skin. "Please, honey. Let me show you how it can be between us. Kiss me again."

Felicity wavered. His rich, gravelly voice poured over her head like thick molasses, drowning her in liquid sweetness that penetrated her pores and set fire to her senses. A man with such a voice should be banned, she thought. He ought not be allowed to speak to susceptible women.

"You're a beautiful, passionate woman," he whispered, bending toward her. "We could make music together that would outclass anything the best musicians could play."

Felicity came back to herself abruptly and stepped back. "Sorry. As I told you before, I'm completely tone-deaf. Even my mother admits I can't carry a tune."

"Felicity, wait. Don't go. Please come back."

Felicity made sure his last sentence was addressed to the closing door. She slammed it shut and shoved a chair beneath the doorknob for good measure.

She gasped for breath and clasped a hand over her pounding heart. She staggered toward the couch and collapsed upon it.

She bent forward and pressed her forehead against her knees. Aaron wanted to be a country musician, and she'd better not forget the fact. Now that he knew she was Becky Lozano's daughter, he was coming on exactly as she'd expected. The question was how long could she resist him? She'd never been tempted like this before, not even by handsome, smooth-talking Gary Carlisle.

She heard the pounding start again and almost moaned aloud with dismay. Every nail he drove seemed to cement the relationship Felicity preferred to think was nonexistent, but she didn't dare open the door and chase him off. She'd probably wind up in his arms again.

She reminded herself he didn't care anything about her as a woman. After all, he hadn't pretended to even like her until he found out she was Becky Lozano's daughter. She ignored the fact that he had kissed her in his barn at the barbecue—that didn't count. He probably kissed a lot of women. A man didn't necessarily have to like a woman in order to want to kiss her. Did he?

Well, he might have fooled Becky with his concerned act, but he certainly couldn't fool Becky's daughter. Felicity had too much experience with would-be country musicians.

Later that afternoon, she answered the kitchen phone, figuring it was a summons to Aaron's house for supper.

"My goodness," Becky said mildly. "Aren't we snappish today. What are you doing, baby?"

"I'm sorting through one-million moldy old magazines, that's what I'm doing. Where are you, Mama?"

"I'm in Tulsa, sugar. Me and Randy gotta do a big show tonight."

Felicity viewed this information with a jaundiced eye and mentally calculated the distance of Tulsa, Oklahoma, from Foxe, Texas. "Shouldn't you be rehearsing?"

"We've already rehearsed," Becky said cheerfully. "Now I want you going next door to Aaron's house for supper tonight. You hear me?"

"Yes, Mama." There was no way she was eating at Aaron's house, but she didn't need to tell Becky that.

"I've already told him to feed you some of that good home-grown beef of his." She digested Felicity's lack of protest and added, "I hope you ain't thinkin' Aaron is anything like that nasty, ol' Gary Carlisle, baby. You can take it from your mama, he ain't."

"No, Mama," Felicity said.

Becky probably didn't know about Aaron's aborted career. At the moment, Felicity didn't feel up to telling her.

"Aaron would never dream of endangerin' my baby's life again with some wicked scheme just to make himself look heroic," Becky continued.

"No, Mama."

"Well, I can see you ain't gonna be sensible about this, and I ain't no matchmakin' mama, so I'll just say this," Becky said. "Accept the man's hospitality, baby. He wants to make it up to you, so why not let him?"

Felicity hung up, doubly resolved not to go anywhere near Aaron. He had spent the entire morning driving nails into loose boards on her house. Apparently, he was very serious about reviving his singing career.

Felicity bathed and put on a white denim skirt and a fringed blue western shirt with a pair of white boots. A clothing saleswoman had to consider herself on display at all times, so she inserted a pair of dangling silver and turquoise earrings and slipped on a matching bracelet. Her only other jewelry was a wide, leather belt with a silver and turquoise buckle.

The telephone rang. "Yes, Mama?"

A deep, rich chuckle answered her. "Sorry," Aaron said. "I was calling to invite you to supper tonight. Polly's cooking chicken-fried steak and mashing real potatoes."

Felicity's mouth watered, but she refused to give in. "Thanks, but I'm busy tonight."

"Come on, honey," Aaron coaxed. "You'll never get anything nearly as good as Polly's chicken-fried steak."

"I'm sure it's very good," Felicity said. "But I've got several errands to run this evening, so I can be home tomorrow while the man finishes covering the well and the roofer comes out to check the roof."

"You still have to eat," Aaron said, mildly. "How about a few meals at my expense?"

"Not tonight, thank you."

Obviously, Aaron was unused to hearing the word no, but Felicity repeated it until he gave up. She grabbed her purse and truck keys, stepped out the front door and locked it, then glared at the house next door.

Aaron's blue truck wasn't there, but then, she hadn't expected it to be. The man had to work sometime. Car dealerships didn't run themselves.

She refused to recognize the slight letdown she felt upon realizing Aaron wasn't present to admire her outfit. It was ridiculous. After all, Aaron wasn't likely to patronize The Cosmic Cowgirl Boutique.

However, the women working in a store that sold cell phones might like her clothes. Felicity had noticed an electronics store on the main highway that ran through town, and she needed a cell phone that would work in this town.

She drove there and went in, pleasantly conscious of every eye in the store turning her way, and walked up to the display of cellular phones. As a saleswoman, she had always owned the latest model Blackberry or smart phone, and it gave her perverse pleasure to choose an inexpensive little cell phone with basic text and phone service, since that was all she really needed for the next two weeks. Becky would be happy and so would the sales staff at

Cosmic Cowgirl. Everyone could get in touch with her easily for as long as she remained in Foxe.

She waited while the young man running the phone center set up the phone service and rang up her ticket. He divided his attention between her and her phone.

"Don't I know you?" he asked, when he presented her at last with her new phone.

"I don't think so." She gave him her most professional smile. "I just arrived in town a few days ago."

"You were at the Whitaker Chevrolet barbecue," he said.

"Yes, I was."

"Everyone was talking about you." His admiring gaze ran over her from head to toe.

"I hope so." She produced a Cosmic Cowgirl business card and handed it to him. "If you have any female friends or family who enjoy western clothes, have them look us up online."

He stared at the card a moment then gazed dreamily on her once more. "Trust old Aaron Whitaker to pick a lady with real class."

Chapter 7

Felicity got back in her truck, steaming. If she denied being Aaron's lover, that would cement the idea in people's heads for sure. She would like to bang her purse over Aaron's head, after she loaded it with a brick.

She caught sight of Whitaker Chevrolet as she neared the freeway. Rows of cars and trucks reflected the fierce blaze of the late afternoon sun. She ought to go find that brick right now, then march in there and let him have it.

She surprised herself by turning suddenly into the dealership's entrance, but she didn't question her own actions until she had climbed out of her own Dodge pickup and felt the heat radiating up from the concrete beneath her feet.

She walked slowly down a row of gleaming new trucks and argued with herself. Telling herself a cowgirl needed to keep up with what Chevrolet had to offer in the way of trucks was such an obvious lie that she could not coax herself into accepting it for long.

She should get back in her own truck and flee. But since she was here, she reasoned, she might as well look over the stock. Aaron never needed to know she had been here.

"Well, lookee here." A rangy young man came toward her from between two new trucks, trailed by a saleswoman who tried in vain to snag his arm. He wore a wide, brown cowboy hat, a large silver belt buckle, and a pair of boots with high heels. Felicity figured if he wasn't a rodeo star, he fancied himself one.

"It's gotta be the barrel-racing champ of Southeast Texas. Hello there, honey," the man added.

"You get on out of here, Jake," the saleswoman accompanying him said. "You're drunk."

"Shut up, Meggie," Jake said. "I got better business than trucks to transact. This cute little heifer and me's got a date at the nearest rodeo arena."

Felicity smiled at the woman. "That's right. Jake and I have a date to discuss a fine little life insurance policy I just happen to be selling."

Jake's hazy eyes focused on her. "Life insurance?"

"That's right. Whenever I go out with someone who drinks, I take the precaution of insuring his life in my favor. That way, if he smashes up his vehicle and causes any damages to my person, I'm fairly compensated." She fished around in the depths of her saddle-shaped purse. "I sell insurance. I just happen to have a fantastic little policy right here from Cow Country Mutual that would be just right for these circumstances."

"Excuse me, ma'am." Jake's hazy blue eyes focused on her purse with fascinated horror. "Just remembered. Got a business appointment in five minutes.

Felicity smiled with friendly understanding. "Listen, Jake, if I can ever help you with any of your insurance needs, here's my card." She produced a Cosmic Cowgirl business card.

Jake fled down a row of gleaming trucks before she could hand him the card.

"Beautifully done," Aaron said from behind her. "Have you ever actually sold insurance?"

Felicity turned slowly. He had appeared out of nowhere and leaned against the shining red hood of an extended cab pickup. He wore jeans that hugged his long legs and a short-sleeved, pale blue western shirt that was open at the neck. He looked like something she'd love to get her hands on.

The moment that thought crossed her mind, Felicity decided retreat was the better part of valor. "As a matter of fact, I have. But I prefer a tangible product I can point to, like a tractor."

"I'll bet you could sell drinking water to mermaids." Aaron took her arm to prevent her from escaping down the same row of trucks as Jake. "I'll take over here, Megan."

Felicity balked. "You'd better leave me with Megan. At the moment, I'm just admiring the stock."

"I can understand why you chose that flashy Dodge of yours," Aaron said smoothly. "But you'll find Chevrolets are the truck of choice for true Texas cowgirls." He flashed his slow, charm-loaded smile. "Allow me to direct your attention to the features a working cowgirl such as yourself will find most useful."

"Oh, spare me." Felicity tried to remove her arm from his grip. "For your information, I chose that Dodge because the color complements my skin. I'm a fall." She knew Aaron would probably have never heard of grouping women's proper color palettes into seasons.

"A what?"

"See there? You'd better turn me over to Megan. I'll bet she knows what kind of truck to show a fall."

Megan, who had spotted another shopper, glanced over her shoulder and grinned. "Show her that turquoise stepside with the mud tires, Aaron. It's a color made for falls."

Aaron took the opportunity to study Felicity's face. "You don't look like fall to me. You look like summer, the way a true cowgirl should."

"True." Megan lingered a moment, gazing longingly upon Felicity's western whites. "I've never seen clothes like those around here before."

"You can get them online." All saleswoman again, Felicity reached into her purse and produced a card. "My shop, The Cosmic Cowgirl, does a lot of online business. And if you're ever in Nashville, be sure and stop in for a look."

Megan took the card, looked Felicity's clothes over with an avaricious gleam in her eyes, and walked dreamily away. Satisfied that she'd landed another customer, Felicity pretended to study a bronze stepside truck. Anything to keep from noticing Aaron, who was smiling appreciatively.

"I hope your shop stocks lots of those outfits," he said. "You're the best advertisement a western store could have."

Felicity ran her fingers over the bronze finish. Aaron stood entirely too close. She fancied she could feel the heat of his body and sense the way his pulse beat rhythmically beneath his tanned wrists. No doubt that was why her own pulse raced along at ninety miles an hour.

"We keep a large inventory," she said.

She was in trouble. Aaron's deep, rough voice alone shook her resolve. She reminded herself again his voice was the major reason she needed to exercise caution. She must have been crazy to stop here.

"You aren't going to make anything easy, are you?" Aaron stepped closer to her.

"Make what easy?" She edged away and casually adjusted the truck's side-view mirror to avoid catching his eye. "I keep on telling you. I'm very satisfied with my truck, but it's possible I may be interested in a Chevrolet in the future."

"I would never have gone off the deep end the way I did if I hadn't been attracted to you the instant I first saw you," he said.

Felicity felt jolted, from the heels of her boots to the leather hair clasp on top of her head. Even though she had expected him to come on to her, she had expected a more devious approach. Anything other than this straightforward declaration. She turned to look at him then wished she hadn't. The moment her gaze made contact with his, everything inside her melted.

Fortunately, the sales training seminars she had attended over the years enabled her to present a smiling facade in the face of the utmost mental confusion. But she couldn't think of a single thing to say that didn't sound fatuous and silly.

Taking her hand, he said, "But I would still like to paddle you for making me think you knew how to ride a horse."

Felicity's eyes widened with indignation and she removed her hand from his clasp. "It was all your fault, and you know it."

He laughed as if pleased. "You're right, it was. I had a powerful hankering to see you on Rhyolite in one of those fancy outfits of yours. But if I'd known you weren't a rider, I'd have been satisfied just looking at you standing beside Rhyolite."

Felicity tossed her head back. The strands of silver and turquoise at her ears danced in the sun and threw flashes of light on his blue shirt. "Now that you mention it, an ad campaign featuring you and your horse, with a model out front in one of our best outfits would probably sell more clothes than all the cards I can pass out. Maybe we can work out some sort of trade."

"Actually, you're the best advertisement going for that shop of yours. You and Rhyolite would make a perfect team."

"I'm not a model." Felicity looked him over. "Whoever heard of a western model with metal stuff on her teeth? But I have a good model on the books, and I'll bet the two of you would make an even better team. When it comes to selling clothes, of course," she added quickly, when Aaron eyed her askance.

"Your braces look like jewelry for teeth," he said. "Maybe you should hire out as a model for the American Dental Association."

Jewelry for teeth? Felicity regarded him thoughtfully. The man was a master of seduction when it came to words. Thank goodness she knew what he really wanted.

Although the hot, humid air seemed to quiver with emotion, Aaron made no move to get too close, and his voice calmed her further. Then she looked into his eyes and felt as if she had made contact with some powerful force that shook her all the way down to her white cowgirl boots.

"How did you come to injure your mouth?" he asked. "From what your mother said, I gathered you were thrown from a horse into something. I've heard of broken bones, but this is the first I've ever heard of a mouth injury."

"Oh, I didn't just get thrown," she said with studied nonchalance. "My horse jumped a fence, and I flew over his head and right into a fence post, lips leading."

The last thing she wanted to talk about right now was Gary Carlisle. Felicity sighed and walked down the row of trucks, absently stopping to stroke her fingers across a shining green hood. What would Aaron say if she just told him the truth?

Aaron followed. "What made you try to jump a fence in the first place if you weren't an experienced rider?"

"Actually, that was the first time I'd ever been on a horse." She shrugged and pretended to study huge mud tires on another new truck. "I guess I can say that I've now spent a grand total of ten minutes on a horse's back. Five minutes then, and five minutes yesterday."

"Then what on earth made you try to jump a fence?" he demanded.

Felicity heard the exasperation in his tone and faced him with flashing eyes. "I didn't try to jump the fence. The horse tried to jump the fence."

Aaron frowned. "Did you give him mixed messages, the way you did with Rhyolite yesterday?"

She glared then looked away. "I never had a chance to give him any messages at all. Suffice it to say, the incident had been planned, but I wasn't supposed to be hurt. I was supposed to be rescued."

Aaron looked absolutely stunned. The expression soothed a little of her irritation.

"What are you talking about?" he asked at last, shaking his head. "I'm not following this at all."

"That's because it's totally unbelievable. It was a stupid incident, and I'd rather forget it. What a beautiful truck." Felicity focused gratefully on a turquoise pickup, which sat high above the ground on over-large tires. "I've never seen one that color before."

"It's a truck made for you," Aaron said. "This is the one Megan says was made for falls, whatever they are. Now I want to know what happened and how you hurt your mouth."

It was that voice of his that made her behave like a jellyfish, she decided wryly. She just couldn't bring herself to tell a man with a voice like that to bug off, even if the voice constituted the chief reason for her wariness. She might as well tell him the whole unbelievable tale. Perhaps then he'd realize he had no chance of fooling her into thinking he cared about her.

"I dated a nice-looking man in Nashville about a year ago," she said. "He claimed he was a computer expert, but I found out later he was waiting tables in a restaurant and playing lead guitar in a country band while he was waiting to be discovered."

Aaron's navy gaze narrowed on her. "Gary Carlisle, I presume. You must have cared a lot for him."

"Not really." She shrugged and minutely examined the truck's hood. "It was too early for that, but maybe I could have cared if he hadn't tried to speed things up." She walked around to peer in at the dashboard. "To make a long story short, it wasn't me he cared about. His only real concern was his career as a country-western musician."

"So what happened?" Aaron asked, regarding her steadily.

"He wanted to take me to bed. Failing that, he wanted me under obligation to him even if he had to pretend he wanted to marry me." Felicity shrugged and looked down the line of new vehicles. The late afternoon sunlight gleaming off their finishes almost blinded her. "We had a few dates, and when none of the above came to pass as fast as he wanted, he decided to jump-start matters."

Aaron's wry half-smile melted her insides.

"I can't say I blame him," he said. "A man can get impatient when the woman he wants drags her heels."

"If I thought he really wanted me, maybe he would have gotten somewhere," Felicity said. "Unfortunately, I was left with the opposite impression."

"What did he do to cause that?"

She shot him a swift glance from beneath her lashes. "It was a collection of little things that are hard to explain, but added together, they left me with the impression that he really didn't find me attractive at all."

For instance, Gary Carlisle hadn't kissed her more than three or four times during their grand total of four dates, and his kisses had impressed her more as "duty" kisses rather than kisses of genuine affection or attraction.

That realization caused her to pause. Aaron had already kissed her more than Gary had during their entire month of dating. What was more, Aaron's kisses lit all her fires and rang all her bells. Surely this attraction could not be one-sided.

She forced her mind back to her story. "He invited me to spend a day horseback riding and picnicking with friends on a dude ranch outside of Nashville." Felicity strolled around the truck and studied its lines scrupulously. "It sounded like a lot of fun."

"Did he know you'd never ridden a horse before?"

"As a matter of fact he did, because I told him. My horse was supposed to be a gentle mare that never moved faster than a walk. Instead, it turned out to be a mare that had been trained for the circus." She almost laughed at his disbelieving expression. "When someone gave the signal, the horse would jump a barrier from almost a standstill position."

"What?"

"I had a little difficulty with the idea myself." Felicity gave him a commiserating grin. "Anyway, I hadn't been in the saddle more than a few minutes when the friends we were supposed to join further up the trail arrived unexpectedly. One of them was my mother's sister."

"Is that supposed to mean something?" Clearly, Aaron missed the message she thought she was sending.

"Well, yes," she admitted, biting back laughter at his baffled look. "Gary got confused and decided the show would have to start sooner than he'd planned, so he gave the horse the signal. The horse got confused because the fence wasn't where it was supposed to be for her act. She took off and jumped the wrong fence."

"There was a right fence?" Aaron looked at her as if she had grown two heads.

"Yes, and that's what caused all Gary's trouble. His whole plan went haywire when the horse jumped the wrong fence, because Gary wasn't in the right spot to save me the way he'd planned. The next thing I knew, I was lying on the ground with paramedics working on me."

Aaron still had trouble following the tale, which sent her into a spasm of inward laughter. Amazed, she wondered when it had suddenly become so hilarious. She had spent almost a year cringing at the very thought of the incident.

He frowned. "Are you saying this guy planned to have you fall off the horse?"

"Yes, he did, but to give him credit, he had planned to catch either me or the horse in a noble and just-in-time rescue." She shot him another glance and struggled to maintain a straight face. "It should have been a piece of cake. There should have been a lot of fuss made over the hero, and maybe I'd even go to bed with him in an attempt to show my gratitude."

Aaron stared at her in fulminating, disbelieving silence.

"Best of all, Mama was sure to hear about every detail of the heroic rescue from her sister and overflow with gratitude."

Aaron had such a stunned expression on his rugged face, Felicity started to ask if he felt all right.

"That is the craziest thing I've ever heard," he said at last, mildly. "Are you sure of his motive?"

Felicity folded her lips together as well as she could over her braces and nodded vigorously. "Unfortunately for him, Mama got to the bottom of his plan within five minutes of talking to the stable owner about that horse."

"Let me get this straight." Aaron frowned heavily. "This guy wanted you to sleep with him so badly, he arranged an accident so he could rescue you and you'd go to bed with him out of gratitude?"

Felicity met his scowl just before bursting into laughter.

"What's so funny?" Aaron demanded. "You could have been killed by that little stunt."

"No kidding." She leaned against the gleaming turquoise truck fender, still laughing. "What I really love is the idea that he was so overcome with desire, he went through extraordinary plotting and expense to set up the situation."

He regarded her gravely. "I hope you aren't going to tell me that if you hadn't been injured, you might have fallen for that idiot."

"No telling what I might have done," she said, between gusts of laughter. "And his idea was probably spot-on if it had gone as planned. If he had performed a daring rescue, Mama might have reacted just as he hoped."

Aaron shook his head in obvious bewilderment. "I still don't understand what your mother had to do with this. Are you saying he was really interested in her rather than in you?"

Felicity regarded him with pitying amusement. "That's exactly what I'm saying, but not in the way you mean. He was interested in what Mama could do for his career."

"*What?*" He was stunned. "Are you trying to tell me this lunatic set you up so your mother would fast-forward his singing career out of gratitude?"

"That's what he hoped," Felicity agreed. "Or so Mama said. She was so mad it took me almost a week to get any sense out of her. It wasn't until he called me one night and begged me to call her off that I finally figured out what was going on."

"I can't believe this." Aaron said. "He had the nerve to ask you to rescue him?"

"Yes, he did. Mama had sicced her lawyer and a private detective on him, not to mention the police. He was in hiding."

"I should think he was." Aaron scowled. "I'd like to get my hands on that jerk."

"So would Mama, and she actually had that private detective out hunting him," Felicity informed him, chuckling. "That little stunt derailed his career for good, and that's what really frosts him. He knows that Mama will do anything she can to ruin his chances. He won't even be able to sing a solo at church if she has anything to say about it."

Aaron's eyes narrowed. "Are you telling me this nut is still calling you?"

"I haven't heard from him in a couple of months, actually." She wiped tears of laughter from her eyes. "The last time he asked me to call off the dogs, or else."

"He said that?"

"Begging and pleading didn't work, so now he's switching to threats. Not that it matters. Mama has informed me that there isn't a thing in the world I can say that will stop her from raking Gary over the coals. If and when she finds him, of course."

"I'm glad you think it's so amusing," Aaron said, still frowning. "That guy ought to be in jail."

"Actually, it was chiefly my pride that was injured," Felicity said. "Along with my vanity, of course. I looked like I'd been in the boxing ring with Joe Frazier for a while there. And Gary isn't really a dangerous man. He's just desperate. In all his planning, I don't think he expected anything like what happened."

"If he's still calling you, he's dangerous." Aaron looked menacing, the way he frowned and clenched his fists. "I don't like that. He has no business wanting you to straighten out the fiasco he caused, especially after you were injured because of him."

"There's nothing he can do to me," Felicity felt obliged to point out. "I blocked him from calling my cell phone and my friends at the shop know not to share any information about my whereabouts."

"A guy who would set up a scene like that is a wild card," Aaron said, his voice a low, deep rumble. "He could try to follow you or something. Who knows what he might do?"

"I know. Believe me, I'm very careful."

"Is your mother aware that he has called you?"

"What do you think?" She could just imagine telling Becky that Gary Carlisle had contacted her.

"Never mind." His gaze met hers, and Felicity felt that look all the way to her toes. "She'd probably hire you a bodyguard."

"She would. I'd never be able to get any work done."

Aaron grinned. "I'd kind of like to hire one for you myself. This guy is a lunatic."

Aaron made her feel delicate and precious; challenged in a purely feminine way she'd never before experienced. And she felt desired, pursued and beautiful. She had to hand it to Aaron. He had Gary Carlisle beat, hands down, when it came to making her feel he wanted her; and she was letting him get to her. Why else would she have told him about that embarrassing incident with Gary?

Aaron studied her. "Maybe I should appoint myself your bodyguard. I'd smash that guy's head into the same fence post you ran into."

"I'd love to see that done, believe me." Felicity thought it prudent to change the subject. "This really is a beautiful truck.

I wish I'd seen it before I bought my Dodge." She ran her hand lovingly over the turquoise finish.

Aaron grinned at her. "For you, honey, we can arrange a trade-in that'll be to your advantage. Want to take her for a test drive?"

Felicity studied the truck longingly, glanced at her watch, and wished she hadn't stopped in at Whitaker Chevrolet. She stood in way too much danger of falling for the owner and CEO.

"That color would go so well with my jewelry," she murmured thoughtfully.

"Now I've heard it all," Aaron said, grinning. "That's the most feminine, girlish reason I've ever heard for buying a new truck."

"A truck is a cowgirl's number one accessory,' Felicity agreed. "White looks so stylish and goes with almost everything. I have to admit, I never even stopped to consider turquoise. Obviously, that was a major oversight on my part."

"Obviously," he agreed, grinning appreciatively. "But before you buy, you've got to drive it and kick its tires. You wouldn't want me to think you know nothing about trucks, would you?"

Felicity shrugged. "I know as much about trucks as I do about horses."

"Oh, well, in that case…"

"Don't choke yourself trying not to laugh. It's a matter of image. In the end, that's what I'm selling—image."

"In that case," Aaron said, "let me get the keys for this beauty and take you for a test drive."

"I really do have to leave," Felicity said and gave the truck one last, longing look.

Before he could push any further, Aaron was called to his office. Felicity took the opportunity to make her escape. She drove swiftly down the highway and turned down a side street that led to the real estate office she had chosen to list the house with.

No doubt about it, the sooner she got that house cleaned out and on the market, the sooner she could clear out of Foxe.

She was in deep, deep trouble, she told herself as she parked her truck. Aaron had actually succeeded in convincing her that he was interested in her, not in what Becky Lozano could do to resurrect his career as a country singer. At the moment, she wasn't sure which was worse: Aaron wanting her for herself, or Aaron wanting to use her as a means of building his career as a singer.

She was sure of only one thing—Aaron had one thing going for him that no other man had ever managed: whether or not he wanted her, she wanted him.

Chapter 8

Aaron left his office in the late afternoon and drove home, thinking hard. The way he saw it, his first hurdle involved getting Felicity to dine with him. If she wouldn't come to his home, then he would just have to take her out.

Obviously, that would take some doing. He wouldn't be able to simply extend an invitation. She probably thought he wanted to take her out in order to bring himself to Becky Lozano's notice—he had to admit she had reason.

He frowned again, wondering at the gall of that guy, Gary Carlisle. How crazy was that, trying to enact a phony rescue in order to gain Becky Lozano's help in getting bookings for his band?

In the end, a would-be star had to have talent. Fifty friends in the industry lending their help would not give more than an artificial boost to a career that was not backed by genuine talent and personal drive. Aaron had seen enough to know that during his own stint as a singer.

In fact, he wouldn't put it past Gary Carlisle to have decided Felicity was responsible for the utter destruction of his career. Any guy willing to pull a stunt like that was also capable of blaming the victim for his own failure.

He turned down the long country road that led to his ranch, already pleasantly conscious of a lift in his spirits. The moment his own spread came into sight, he looked a little further down the road toward Felicity's cottage and felt a surge of anticipation when he spotted her truck in the driveway.

He turned in the long driveway that circled in front of his house and followed the branch-off that led to the side of the house and the barn. To his surprise, Felicity, slim and dashing in her long white skirt and fringed shirt, led a small pony toward his barn, accompanied by his two brown labs.

Donatello? Had Felicity taken Donatello from his stall in some sort of effort to get over her fear of horses? Plus, he kept the dogs in the house most of the time. How had they gotten out?

Aaron sat perfectly still, contemplating the possibilities. She could not have been home long. More likely, she had discovered Donatello grazing on her property and was returning the pony to his stall. But how had the pony and the dogs escaped in the first place?

He exited his truck only to be met by Deborah, who burst from the house wild-eyed and frantic.

"The boys," she cried. "I can't find them. They're gone, Aaron!"

"Calm down, Deb," he said gently. "Have you looked in the barn?"

"I haven't had a chance yet," she said, panting, dark hair disheveled. "They were playing in the den not more than half an hour ago. I just got through searching all over the house."

Aaron looked toward the barn, where Felicity reached to pull open the barn door. "I think I know where they—"

Suddenly, all hell broke loose.

Felicity stepped inside the barn and screamed. She vanished into a roiling white fog that erupted from the open barn door like volcanic steam. Donatello, normally a placid, even-tempered pony, reared back, and trotted down the driveway as fast as his short little legs would carry him. The two dogs ran in circles outside the door, barking wildly.

Aaron heard another scream, followed by what sounded like ferocious choking. He raced toward the barn, where the billowing white cloud rolled out the front door like a devouring mist. The barn door stood open, but he could not see anything for the white fog that shrouded the doorway.

He leaped inside, prepared to kill any intruder, but the moment his boot touched the floor, his foot shot out from under him. He rose into the air a good three feet, then fell heavily to the floor on his back and actually slid a few more feet into the room until he crashed into an obstacle.

He couldn't see a thing, but the obstacle was warm and resilient. He sucked in his breath to speak but choked on the white powder filling the air and went into a paroxysm of coughing.

"Fancy meeting you here, Mr. Whitaker," Felicity choked out between coughs.

He could not speak for several minutes.

"What the hell is going on in here?" he wheezed, when he was finally able to speak.

"I was hoping you could tell me." Felicity sat on the floor, covered with the white powder. Her hair shone with white powder and something oily dripped down her blouse.

"Vegetable oil," he exclaimed, identifying the odor at last. "And this white stuff looks like flour. What on earth——?"

"Flour?" Felicity coughed. She sounded as baffled as he was.

They stared at each other through the residual white mist. Felicity looked as though someone had dumped a bucket of flour over her head. Tears streaked down her face from coughing so much. Aaron figured he probably looked much the same.

"Are you all right?" he asked and coughed.

"I think so, but everything that was sore from yesterday is now even sorer." She leaned forward and rubbed the back of her oil-soaked white skirt.

He wiped white powder from his eyes and stared around in search of intruders. "I don't suppose you've got any ideas about how this came about."

"I'm afraid not." She rubbed her elbow and studied the big oil spot on her blouse. "When I got home, I found one of your ponies grazing in my backyard, so I thought I'd just walk him back over.

I opened the barn door and took one step inside and my feet went out from under me. The minute I hit the floor, something landed on my head and this white stuff went in my face and blinded me. Then I breathed it in and nearly choked half to death." She added scrupulously, "I don't know what happened to that poor little pony."

"Don't worry about Donatello. He fled the scene and went right back to your backyard."

He caught sight of a small, plastic bucket lying on the floor and looked up at the small ledge above the barn door. Someone had taken advantage of the architecture to set a trap designed to ensnare the first person to enter the barn.

He studied the plastic bucket again…he had seen it before.

"Someone booby-trapped the door with a bucket of flour," he said. "And to add insult to injury, they also greased the floor."

"But why?" Felicity asked. "It doesn't make any sense."

"Maybe I'd better call the sheriff," Aaron decided. "At the very least, someone is guilty of breaking and entering. Plus you or whoever entered first could have been injured." He looked at the bucket once more. "On the other hand, maybe I'd better check the rest of the barn. The culprit might be hiding in here."

"You're right." Felicity struggled to rise. "You might not want to call the sheriff." She made it to her hands and knees. "This reminds me of something."

Aaron narrowed his eyes and stared down the long aisle. "If you think it's that Carlisle nut, you'd better stay right here while I check the stalls."

"I can't imagine why Gary Carlisle would booby-trap your barn. He's the kind who's a lot more likely to try and bribe me than he is to hurt me."

Aaron ignored this. "Maybe that's why the pony was put to graze in your yard. Carlisle probably knew you'd try and return him to his stall."

"Surely the dogs would have given a warning."

"Maybe, but they're more likely to usher him inside and show him around," Aaron said in dry tones.

He got to his feet very carefully, holding on to the edge of the barn door. Then he bent and lifted Felicity to her feet. One foot shot out from beneath her the moment she put her weight on her feet and she clutched his arms. He held her steady, careful not to move.

"Thanks. Every time I tried to get up, I slipped back into the oil." She looked down at herself. "I hope there's a really good dry cleaning place in town. Maybe they can save this outfit, although I doubt it."

He held her, amused that she was hardly aware of his proximity while she assessed the damage to her clothes. "The dry cleaner is just down the highway from my dealership."

She looked up, strongly resembling an owl covered in snow. The moment she did, he drew her in and kissed her. "I came out here to invite you to dinner, Felicity," he said solemnly. "But it looks like it'll have to be a late dinner. It's going to take an hour or two for both of us to get the vegetable oil and flour out of our hair."

Felicity stared at him as if dazed by the kiss. "I may not be able to move after busting my poor bones on this hardwood floor. They still haven't recovered from landing on your front lawn yesterday."

"In that case, allow me to recommend an hour in my whirlpool tub. Guaranteed to ease your soreness and restore mobility to frozen joints."

"Thanks. I may have to take you up on it if I hope to ever move again." She released her grip on his arms and gingerly took a step. "That's assuming I can make it out of here without going down again." She grabbed the barn door and held on for dear life.

"Stay just outside the door," Aaron commanded. "Let me have a look around before you go home, just in case."

To his surprise, she remained just outside the barn door as instructed, coughing and gingerly inspecting the oil stains on her clothes while he went back inside. Her uncharacteristic obedience might have been due to the shock of her fall, he told himself, grinning. Or maybe the kiss had affected her as much as it did him.

He went back inside the barn, skirting the big puddle of oil and flour, and headed down the center aisle, where he methodically checked the first two stalls. They were empty, as they should have been, but he didn't know what he'd find further down the row.

Before he could speculate on who had let the pony out of his stall, he heard a loud shriek and thump from behind him.

"Aaron," his sister screamed. "Where are you?"

That was all she managed before she began coughing violently. Between coughs, she tried to call to him again.

"I'm right here, Deb." He turned back and approached cautiously to help her rise from the oil and clouds of flour. "Somebody set a trap to catch whoever came through the barn door first." He managed not to laugh, remembering that Felicity was just outside. "Be thankful you weren't the first."

"What?" Deborah coughed some more. "Is this what happened to Felicity? She was coughing so hard, she couldn't answer me when I asked if she'd seen the boys. Aaron, they've disappeared again." She clutched his arm. "Tony called and I was almost frantic." She sucked in her breath on another cough. "I thought they were playing with their toy cars in the den, but when I went to check on them, they were gone."

"Don't worry, Deb." Aaron knew better than to grin, but laughter was building slowly and inexorably inside him now that he realized Felicity's ex-boyfriend had not set the trap. "I have a feeling I know just where to find them."

Deborah sagged with relief. "Thank God. I've been so worried." She struggled to stand, and he had to lead her to a dry portion of the wooden floor. "Where are they?"

"Stay out front with Felicity," Aaron said. "I'll go get them."

Deborah craned her neck to inspect her bottom. "Mercy, Aaron. I'm covered with salad oil."

The shocked surprise in her voice must have reached Felicity. She stood in the barn door looking at the big, oily spots on Deborah's navy trousers. The same laughter shaking Aaron seemed to be building inside her, judging from the expression on her slender, flour-dusted face.

"I guess this means you don't know anything about the barnyard oil spill," Felicity said between coughs. "Or the bucket of flour that fell on my head the minute I stepped inside?"

"Oil and flour?" Deborah sounded as though she had awakened and found herself in an alternate universe. "Is that what this is?" Understanding suddenly dawned on her pale, beautiful face. "Oh, no...the boys." She gripped Aaron's arm. "When their father called, they must have heard and decided their ghost was after them again. Oh, Aaron, what am I going to do?"

Felicity gave way. Peels of laughter poured from her throat. Aaron joined in, and Deborah stared helplessly at the two of them.

"I can't wait to find out what the flour was for." Choking, Felicity collapsed against the edge of the open barn door. "What I want to know is why no one has yet explained to them that ghosts can't be caught with these corporal methods."

"You look like a ghost yourself," Aaron teased. "When you appeared on the floor in a puff of smoke, I thought I'd stumbled onto the set of a vampire movie." He beckoned the two of them to follow him. "What do you say we go find them? I have to admit, I'm curious about the flour too."

"Oh, Felicity, I don't know how to apologize," Deborah said, distressed. "Aaron, you've got to do something. This ghost thing has gotten beyond me."

"Don't worry, Deb." Aaron lowered his voice gently. "Our resident ghost expert is here. Maybe she can suggest a way to straighten out this mess."

Felicity grinned. "It's probably a good thing I was the first one in the door. But I'll bet poor little Donatello will never be the same again." She sputtered with laughter and added, "You'll probably have trouble getting him to come inside the barn tonight."

Thanks to the liberal dosage of flour on the floor, she made it across the threshold and skirted the main pool of oil without falling. Once inside, both women followed Aaron down the center aisle as he stopped to check each stall, even though he figured the stall of interest was the smaller stall normally occupied by Donatello.

A blue plastic tarp had been spread over the top of the stall. As they drew closer, Aaron saw that every crack between the boards had been stuffed with straw or cloth, and a blanket had been stuffed in the space beneath the door.

Aaron stood gazing at the stall door in thoughtful silence for a moment. "I wonder what we do now?" he said. "They might have a heart attack if I just pull open the door."

Felicity solved the problem by knocking gently.

"Who…who's out there?" a quavering, young voice asked.

"Your friendly, neighborhood ghost-buster is here to look into your problem," Felicity called. "Open up, Pete. You're safe now. Your Uncle Aaron and your mom are here with me."

"Felicity." The voice was muffled, but unmistakably joyous. "She's here."

The stall occupants fumbled with the wooden door. Seconds later it creaked open and two scared knights in full ghost-busting armor tumbled out and fell upon Felicity.

"Felicity, the ghost almost got us." Joey, teeth chattering, clung to her legs, apparently unaware that Felicity was covered with flour and oil. "We set a trap for him and hid."

Deborah clapped one oil-slicked hand to her forehead, moaned and leaned weakly against the stall. "What on earth am I going to do with them?"

"Did you see our trap, Felicity?" Pete stood before her, kitchen fork at his shoulder, like a soldier before his captain. "We're ready for that old ghost."

Felicity, conscious of Aaron's smothered chuckles, replied gravely, "Yes, Pete, I can see you were." She looked down at herself. "The only problem here is that the trap you set for the ghost works only on people. Ghosts aren't solid like people. They require different methods."

"Oh, but this trap will work for the ghost." Pete gestured eagerly with the fork. "If he comes in the door, he's going to get oil on his feet and fall down and then flour is going to fall on him and make him so we can see him. Then we can let all the air out of him." At this moment, Pete registered Felicity's unusual mode of decoration. He gulped and said weakly, "Uh-oh." The saucepan on his head fell off with a loud clatter when he hung his head.

Deborah buried her face in her hands with another soft moan. "I've told them and told them. There are no such things as ghosts."

"'Uh-oh' is right," Aaron said, with admirable gravity under the circumstances. "You made Felicity fall, and you made your mother and I fall. We could have been hurt. This ghost business has gone far enough, boys."

There was a moment of apprehensive silence.

"Are you going to spank us, Uncle Aaron?" Pete asked bravely.

Joey began to sniff dolefully and clung to Felicity's oily white skirt.

"I have a feeling you'll have been punished enough by the time you've scrubbed all the oil and flour off the barn floor." Aaron stood looking down at the two crestfallen children. Kneeling, he reached for Pete and looked into the boy's face. "Pete, this ghost isn't real. You know that, don't you?"

"But he *is* real," Pete protested earnestly. "He's a real *bad* ghost, Uncle Aaron."

"If you think about it, you'll realize your ghost is actually your fear about why you left your own house and why you haven't seen your dad lately," Aaron said gently.

Deborah gasped but said nothing.

Pete hung his head again, sniffing. Joey buried his face against Felicity's skirt and began to cry.

"When you overheard your mother and me talking about the situation, you jumped to the conclusion that something bad was after you. So you created your ghost as a reason why you had to leave your own house." Aaron reached for Joey and drew him out from behind Felicity. "The worst thing about it is that you're carrying your fear with you. Wherever the two of you go, your fear goes, and so does your ghost."

Pete swallowed, big-eyed. "The ghost is still chasing us?"

"What you're really afraid of is chasing you," Aaron corrected, clasping Pete's shoulder with one big hand. "You don't know what's happened to your dad, and you're afraid to find out. Until you face that fear, you'll keep on hiding in closets and stalls and being afraid to go to bed. Is that what you want? To keep on being afraid?"

Pete grimaced in thought. "How do we find out where Daddy is? Will he make the ghost stop following us?"

"You call him on the telephone," Aaron said. "Ask him when he's coming to see you."

"And when he comes, the ghost will leave?" Joey asked eagerly.

"No, Aaron," Deborah whispered, gesturing wildly. "I'm not ready to confront Tony yet."

"This has gone too far already, Deb." Aaron gently took the two kitchen forks from the little boys and tucked them inside the waistband of his jeans. "If you can't face Tony, that's your business, but unless you want the boys coming up with more outlandish ideas for ghost-fighting, you'll let them get this business with their father straight in their own minds. They have a right to see him."

To his relief, Felicity touched Deborah's shoulder and nodded her agreement. Oddly enough, the Sachitano family seemed to think Felicity was a font of knowledge when it came to ghost-busting. Aaron grinned inwardly and registered sentiments of gratitude for that fact.

"We all have things we're afraid of," Aaron said, tapping Pete's chin with one big finger. "Even grown-ups have things they're afraid to face. But if you don't stop and find out what's really making you so afraid, you'll never be free, and the next thing you know, it turns into something really scary, like your 'ghost.'"

"Was a ghost chasing you, Uncle Aaron?" Joey asked, goggle-eyed.

"It wasn't really a ghost," Aaron said, smiling. "It was a silly and wrong idea I'd taken into my head about what I wanted to do in life. It really had me going until one day, after everything I tried went wrong, I finally had to sit down and face it and see it for what it was. That's when I decided to change careers, and I've been happy ever since."

"But was it a really bad old ghost?" Joey asked again.

Aaron glanced at Felicity, whose face reflected understanding and sympathy. His sister, however, watched him in horrified fascination.

"No, Joey, it wasn't. It wasn't a ghost, and it wasn't even very scary once I sat down and really thought about it." He focused on the little boys once more. "And I think that once you've had a chance to talk to your dad, you'll find that your so-called ghost isn't nearly as scary as you thought. In fact, he might just vanish forever."

"He'll bust," Joey exclaimed, with enthusiasm. "He'll make a big noise and lots of fire."

"Maybe he'll even explode," Pete agreed. "Wow."

The idea clearly found favor with the two children, but it didn't take Aaron long to realize that what the boys really wanted was for the ghost to go out in style, with a burst of loud pyrotechnics as it vanished forever.

He went through the whole thing again with great patience, but either the boys were too young to understand, or their ghost had taken such possession of their minds, they refused to give it up without a proper ceremony. Every time Aaron declared the ghost unreal, the boys countered with proofs of the ghost's existence.

"But he really is real. We heard him, Uncle Aaron," Pete insisted, with great earnestness. "He whispered to us last night, almost all night long."

"Boys, there are no such things as ghosts," Deborah reiterated, for perhaps the tenth time in ten minutes. "And if there were, they couldn't talk to you."

Aaron glanced at Felicity, amused that he found her striking even in her disheveled, flour-covered state. Maybe she knew how to conduct a ghost exorcism.

"What do you mean, he whispered to you?" Felicity asked.

"He talked to us," Joey said. "But we couldn't hear what he was saying."

"Does that mean something was talking very softly, or does it mean it sounded far away?" Felicity went on. "Or do you think maybe it was talking in another language?"

Aaron gave her a warning grimace. He wasn't so sure he wanted the ghost cemented into the boys' imaginations with all those questions, as though it were a real entity.

Deborah shook her head, clearly unable to deal with such an unprecedented situation. "They can't possibly have gotten all this from Jason."

"The ghost was whispering," Pete reiterated. "It sounded sort of soft and squeaky and we could both hear him, but we couldn't understand anything he said."

"You heard an actual voice?" Felicity asked, frowning.

"It was a *ghost* voice." Joey tugged at her skirt. "It was scary, Felicity. We hid under our blankets so he wouldn't see us."

"You say this was last night?" she asked. "How long did you hear the voice?"

"It was hours and hours," Joey assured her. "We were scared he might see us, or we would have sneaked out in the hall to go find Uncle Aaron."

"When did you stop hearing the voice?" Felicity asked.

"It was when the sun came up," Pete said. "Joey was asleep."

"Was not," Joey said.

"Hmmmmm…" Felicity said thoughtfully.

Aaron watched the scene with some amusement and wondered what Felicity meant to suggest for this new wrinkle. Both boys hung on her every word with hope that wrung his heart. Whatever had kept them awake during the night had scared them badly.

Felicity asked a few more questions and discovered that the ghostly whispers—which sounded like rustling newspapers and tiny squeaks—seemed to come from the closet. Moreover, when one of the boys chucked a house slipper at the wall, the sounds had ceased for several moments before resuming.

Deborah frowned. "I can't imagine what that could be."

"This calls for action," Felicity said. "When a ghost starts keeping people up all night, something has got to be done."

"We couldn't agree more. In fact, we're all ears," Aaron said. "What do you suggest?"

"I think I'd better spend the night in the boys' bedroom tonight. I'd like to get a better feel for this particular ghost before we develop a method to deal with him."

Deborah gave her a look of intense gratitude. "I hate to ask that of you, but—"

"Oh, boy," Pete said. "Felicity can have my bed, Uncle Aaron."

"Mine," Joey insisted.

Aaron couldn't believe his luck. Felicity proposed to spend the night in his house, and he hadn't needed to say a word to bring it about. Sometimes, fortune smiled on a man, and said man would be wise not to question fortune. He just wished this ghost thing wasn't the big item on Felicity's mind tonight. He wanted to be the only item on her mind.

But this was a step in the right direction ...

Chapter 9

After changing into a loose-fitting black denim skirt and floaty turquoise gauze blouse, Felicity slung her tote bag over her shoulder and locked the front door behind her. No doubt she had flipped into an alternate reality, but she felt constitutionally incapable of letting those two scared little boys live in terror of their ghost any longer.

She ignored the nagging voice in her head that told her she had already exceeded the limits of her ghost-busting knowledge. Children needed peaceful sleep in order to grow. She was an adult. Therefore, she ought to be able to discover the source of the whispering ghost in their bedroom, so the little boys could sleep again.

Until the next manifestation of their "ghost," that is. So long as they did not understand why their father had vanished from their lives, they would continue finding their own explanations. She had to admire their creativity.

And she was so far gone, she couldn't wait to spend more time with Aaron. When she heard Aaron carefully trying to explain their ghost to the two little boys, something happened inside her heart. She wasn't sure what had happened or why, but she suddenly knew Aaron could be trusted.

She marched across the grass in the warm twilight and made her way to the front door of Aaron's house. On the way, she swatted the little black bugs away from her hair and body.

A grand total of five shampooings had finally rid her hair of the flour and vegetable oil, so she had no intention of allowing any of those black bugs to land anywhere on her. The crust they formed on her truck would be enough trouble to clean.

The two little boys and Aaron's two retrievers waited at the window for her. The moment she came into view, the front door banged open and all four charged out to greet her.

"Felicity, Mama made up my bed with fresh sheets for you," Pete said. "Polly says you need to have the room to yourself, but Joey and I don't want you to be afraid. We can sleep in Joey's bed. Okay, Felicity?"

Joey echoed these same sentiments while Felicity greeted the dogs. The two children, each holding one of her hands, led her to the door, quivering with excitement and bravado.

"That's really very thoughtful of you both, not to mention brave, but the two of you are bound to be pretty sleepy if you didn't sleep last night. Maybe you should sleep in another bedroom, just for tonight."

"We had naps," Joey assured her. "We want to help you chase off that mean old ghost, Felicity."

"We want to see you kill him," Pete said, with bloodthirsty emphasis.

Great. The boys wanted to know for certain the ghost was gone for good. That probably meant some sort of exorcism ceremony.

"Let's go in and see what your mom says." Felicity wondered if the two little boys had spoken to their father yet. "In the meantime, let's see about getting a bottle of garlic powder. We want to be well-armed if the ghost appears tonight."

"Oh, boy." Pete ran toward the kitchen, followed by Joey, presumably to procure a bottle of garlic powder in the kitchen.

She entered with the dogs and shut the front door behind her, grinning. The night promised to be far more interesting than the previous night she had spent sorting through countless mildewed magazines and other assorted trash in search of Becky's songs. In spite of her efforts, the living room still looked like a junk pile, and she was heartily fed up with the smell of musty paper.

"You're here. I didn't hear you knock." Aaron entered the foyer, frowning. "Pete and Joey have been standing at the window waiting for you for the past twenty minutes. Where did they go?"

"They're in the kitchen, putting in a request for a bottle of ghost-busting garlic powder," Felicity noted that he wore black jeans and a black t-shirt that accentuated his broad shoulders and showed his muscular arms. Her heartbeat speeded up accordingly. "It never hurts to be prepared."

"We couldn't get their father on the phone," Aaron said. "He was in meetings all evening. Something's going on with his commercial real estate business, but Deb claims she doesn't know a thing about it." He shrugged and reached out to take her shoulder tote. "Until the boys get a chance to discuss things with Tony, they'll hold onto this ghost idea."

"It's understandable, given that they're so young. Plus, it's perfectly obvious that their cousin Jason has been telling them ghost stories. Naturally, they put the two together." She followed him into a comfortable living room where Deborah sat on the sofa with a book in her hands. "I have to admit, I was impressed with their reasoning in the matter of the ghost trap. I would never have thought of something like that."

She met his laughing dark blue eyes and knew a moment of breathlessness. The man ought to be declared illegal. Off-limits. Forbidden to appear in public, in order to protect impressionable women such as herself. She reminded herself that she wanted the same kind of love her mother had shared with her father. Just because she found Aaron physically attractive —

"I'll tell you a secret," he said. "Neither would I."

Okay, so she found all of him attractive. He still should be outlawed.

"Oh, Felicity, I'm so sorry about everything," Deborah said. "Thank you for coming tonight. The boys are so excited, they probably won't sleep a wink."

"I'm hoping they're still tired from last night," Felicity said. "If we can rid their bedroom of the whispering ghost, I have a feeling most of your troubles will be over."

"All I can say is I hope that's true. I just can't understand where they've gotten this idea of a ghost." Deborah stopped and shook her head. "It just floors me. I've talked to them and talked to them, but all they'll say is that this particular ghost is real."

Felicity laughed at that. "Children have all kinds of peculiar ideas. I think it begins with something they hear then their imaginations go to work on it. When I was a child, I was absolutely certain there was a fairy queen who lived in my closet. My mother had no idea where I came up with the idea."

Aaron motioned for her to sit beside Deborah on the sofa and he relaxed on an easy chair across from them. "Where did you come up with it?"

Felicity tried hard not to stare at him. "I saw a picture of a fairy queen in a story book my mother bought for me." She smiled at Deborah and added, "The fairy queen's attendants all had wings, like the moths that lived in my closet."

"And what did your mother do when she finally figured out the connection?" Aaron asked, grinning.

"She went after the cause, which turned out to be an old wool coat at the very back of the closet." It was no use. Aaron commanded her attention just by his very presence. "Some insect spray took care of any remaining problems."

"Felicity, look. We've got two bottles of garlic powder." Pete scampered in, followed by Joey, and held out a spice bottle that bore the label, "Garlic Powder."

Joey clutched another bottle to his small chest, obviously reluctant to let it out of his hands.

Felicity took Pete's bottle and studied it with approval. "Very good, Pete. This will do nicely. Just in case the ghost gets uppity, you know."

"Not with Felicity on the job, he won't," Aaron said. "I predict a very peaceful night for us all. Don't think for a minute the ghost doesn't know Felicity is here, with garlic powder. I'll be surprised if he makes a single sound tonight."

"It never hurts to be ready." Felicity tucked the bottle into her tote, which Aaron had placed on the floor by her feet. "We're going to set this bottle out on the bedside table, just in case. We want to be prepared for any eventuality."

"Oh, boy." Joey clutched his own bottle of garlic powder. "We'll blast that mean old ghost to smithereens."

"Boys—" Deborah began. She stopped gave Felicity deprecating glance. "Never mind. I can see it won't make a bit of difference."

Aaron shook his head. "This should be a night to remember."

"Don't worry, Uncle Aaron," Joey said, with great earnestness. "Felicity won't let the mean old ghost hurt you."

Aaron stared down into the boy's earnest face. "Believe me, Joey, I'm counting on that." He looked at Felicity and smiled his slow, hot smile. "Why don't the two of you settle down and watch some cartoons on the television while I show Felicity the bedroom and the rest of the house."

Felicity bit her lip and waited while Aaron countered all the boys' arguments for accompanying them and sent them shuffling off to the living room. Wasn't this the sort of situation a sensible woman ought to avoid? Obviously, Aaron wanted to be alone with her, and just as obviously, she ought to avoid being alone with him.

"And now, Miss Clayton, about that tour of the house." He picked up her tote by the strap and held out his other arm. "In case the ghost proves tougher than we think, you might need to know the layout of the place."

"So I'll know where to run and hide?" She rose and took his arm. She would be the first to admit she had left her good sense at home. "Let's just hope we don't run into any more traps your nephews might have set and forgot about."

"If there are any more traps, I don't know what I'll do," Deborah said. "Aaron, maybe I should take them to a counselor."

"Don't worry about it yet, Deb," Aaron said in his soothing, graveled tones. "Felicity may solve the whole problem for us tonight."

"I'm hoping for a branch scraping on the window or something of the sort." Felicity dragged her mind back to the ghost problem with difficulty. "If I can find out what it is, then Aaron can fix it or put a stop to it, and half your problem is solved right there."

Deborah gave her a look of profound gratitude. "I do hope you're right. I can't thank you enough for being willing to come over and look into this. The boys have such faith in you."

Felicity smiled back. "Then let's all hope the ghost appears tonight, so I can conduct a proper exorcism."

Aaron escorted her out of the room and down the hall toward the kitchen. "That's what I like about you, Miss Clayton. You have an intrepid spirit. Nothing scares you, not even a bad old ghost that terrorizes little boys."

Felicity's nerves jittered with awareness of the most pleasant sort. All her senses focused upon Aaron, especially when he reached out to open the door to the kitchen. She watched his muscles flex when he opened the door for her and tried to keep her mind on what he was saying.

"Actually, I spook out as much as anyone when I hear strange sounds in the night," she managed. "Let's just hope I can identify the cause of the sounds right away. Otherwise, you may see a streak shooting down your hall and out your front door." She entered the large, well-lit kitchen and reached out to touch one of the granite countertops. "Or maybe I'll just run in here." Pointing to a ceramic bowl filled with several garlic pods, she added, "The ghost repellent is already in place."

"Well, Miss Clayton." Aaron set her tote on the table and turned her gently to face him. "You seem to have recovered nicely from the incident this afternoon. Are you sure you're all right?"

She wasn't fine. She was undergoing a core meltdown. "I'm fine. Just a little bruised on the hip where I landed. I soaked in my bathtub for an hour."

"Maybe you should let me rub the injured area down with arnica." His hand dropped to rest on her injured hip, while his other hand flattened on the center of her back and drew her inexorably toward him. "Arnica does wonders for bruises."

Felicity lost all power of speech. She stared into his navy eyes, scarcely breathing.

"In fact, if you'd like an all-over body massage, you'll find I'm very skilled at the art," he said and kissed her.

Felicity melted. The seductive, gravelly voice, combined with his big, all-male body, and that intense dark-blue stare added up to a single knock-out punch that lifted her to nirvana. Once she felt his lips on hers, she was out for the count. He could have undressed her and made love to her on the kitchen table without a single reprimand from her.

A few moments later, he said, breathing hard, "Let's walk out to the barn. I want to show you how well Joey and Pete cleaned up the flour and oil."

Breathless herself, she gasped, "I'd love to see it."

How original, she thought, with what remained of her good sense. She was largely ignorant of such things, but instinctively knew Aaron's intentions.

Fortunately for what remained of her scruples and good sense, Pete came looking for them.

"Felicity, are you ready to go to bed yet?" the child asked. "We're supposed to go to sleep now, but Mom says we can stay up until you're ready. She says that after the day you've had, you'll probably be ready pretty soon."

She hastily turned out of Aaron's arms. "Your mom is right, Pete. I'll be ready for bed as soon as your uncle finishes showing me around the house."

While Aaron sent Pete back to the living room, the cell phone she had tucked in her skirt pocket trilled, annoying her considerably. She had told Becky about the ghost and her current efforts to eradicate it. Why was Becky calling now, when she was sure to interrupt the sort of scene she wanted to encourage between her daughter and Aaron?

But the caller turned out to be Felicity's right-hand woman and manager of the Cosmic Cowgirl, Suzi Marlowe, with an unwelcome message.

"That same man called here again," Suzi shared worriedly. "He's called about three times so far and wants to know when you'll be back, where are you, etc., etc. Just thought you ought to know."

"Thanks, Suzi. Just make sure nobody tells him anything." She clicked off the phone and despite her best efforts to hide her dismay, found Aaron regarding her thoughtfully. "Yes?"

"It's Gary Carlisle, right? He's still looking for you." Aaron took her hand and led her down the hall to show her the bedrooms. "What do you think stirred him up?"

"It wouldn't surprise me to find out he has a contact in the Nashville Police Department who's keeping him updated on the status of the charges against him," Felicity said. "Mama is still hot on his trail." She sighed and added, "It's no good talking to her. The only thing that'll calm her down is time, and time is not on his side. He can't get a job or even drive around without risking arrest, so I can't blame him for being upset."

"He should have thought of that before he arranged that stupid stunt of his," Aaron said, frowning. "Sorry, honey. I'm with your mother on this one."

"Like I said, I won't get anywhere talking to her, so he's wasting his time calling me." Felicity shrugged. "His best bet is to move, preferably to another country, but at least to some state she rarely performs in…like Alaska."

Aaron chuckled and opened the door to a plainly furnished bedroom that boasted two twin beds with identical blue bedspreads. "This is your bedroom for the night. I'm putting the boys across the hall."

Felicity entered the room while Aaron placed her tote on one of the beds. The closet door stood open, revealing a neat array of small boys' shirts and jackets. She peeped inside and saw nothing unusual about the shoes on the closet floor or the suitcases tucked away in the back.

"I don't suppose there's a tree just outside the window, or a bush with long branches?" she asked.

"Not a thing," Aaron said, smiling. "But I've got faith in your ability to get to the bottom of this, Miss Clayton." He took her into his arms. "I've got faith in you, period."

He kissed her, and Felicity found her arms going around his neck with swift, unquestioning desire. How and when had this happened? She wasn't sure, but she had little doubt as to how it would end. In fact, she looked forward to making love with Aaron Whitaker with so much enthusiasm, it scared her.

She trembled in his arms and wondered if now would be a good time to point out the proximity of a bed.

"Are you going to bed yet, Felicity?" Joey called from the hall.

Aaron let her go, grinning wryly. "I was just showing her the bedroom, Joey. I'm sure she's about ready for a good night's rest, after falling into your ghost trap today."

Felicity looked at the bed, resigned. If she couldn't make love with Aaron, then she might as well get some sleep, and if she was really lucky, she would solve the mystery of the ghost at some time during the night.

"The sooner we turn out all the lights, the sooner we can get started in solving our ghost problem," she agreed. "Professional ghost-hunters who go to bed early have a better chance of getting the ghost."

•••

"Felicity. Felicity."

She jolted awake. Joey had crawled into bed beside her and shook her arm frantically.

"He's here," Pete whispered. He climbed on the other side of the bed. "Can you hear him?"

Felicity listened, but the bedroom was silent except for the rapid panting of the frightened little boys.

"What are you two doing in here?" she asked. "You're supposed to be asleep in the bedroom across the hall."

"We wanted to be sure you were okay and see if you had caught the ghost yet," Pete explained. "Then, just as we came in, we heard him."

She sat up. A night light at the far end of the bedroom cast its glow over that corner. She turned her head and noted that her little clock said it was three in the morning. The room appeared empty except for the three occupants of Felicity's bed.

"Maybe he heard us." Pete shivered and moved a little closer to Felicity.

"Shhhhh." Joey clutched her arm.

She wasn't sure, but she thought she heard something move in the quiet bedroom. She leaned forward and listened for all she was worth. The lace that lined the neck of her sleep-shirt almost fluttered with the force of her own rapid breathing.

A strange scraping sound came from the closet. Felicity felt the hair on the back of her neck lift gently and admitted to herself that there was something truly spooky about the faint whispering sounds coming from the closet. She had hoped to discover a branch brushing against the window during the wee hours of the night, or maybe even hear the whispering of a distant radio or television set, but this sound indicated life and movement.

Something alive occupied that closet.

Or something that had once been alive and was now dead. The hair on the back of her neck levitated a little higher.

Joey whimpered.

Pete clutched her arm. "It's the ghost."

They sat in dead silence for a few minutes, listening intently. The boys' terrified breathing sounded so loud in the dead stillness of the night, Felicity wondered how any ghost that wasn't deaf could keep from hearing them.

Strange whispering sounds, followed by a peculiar squeak, issued from the closet. Felicity listened and stared toward the dark, open closet in the semi-darkness. No wonder the two little boys had thought the ghost was talking to them.

More whispering issued forth, followed by a weird and rhythmic scratching sound.

The closet door stood open. She had opened it herself, while the two little boys watched, on the grounds that the ghost wouldn't be able to hide in there. The idea had sounded good in a fully lit bedroom full of people, but in the darkness, with only the protection of two small boys, Felicity seriously considered leaping up and slamming the closet door shut, as she sped by on her way out the bedroom door.

She reached for the lamp on the bedside table. A little more light on the subject …

More squeaking and whispering came from amidst the clothes and shoes, along with the rustling of a newspaper or paper bag. The boys clutched her arms hard enough to cut off her circulation and plastered themselves against her.

"Okay, ghost. Come out of there with your hands up," she said to the closet in a low, shaky voice. "We should warn you, we're armed."

The sounds ceased. They waited with bated breath, staring at the black void of the open closet door. Felicity gathered her wits and prepared herself to face down whatever was lurking in the closet. What else could she do, with the two little boys expecting her to save them?

While she climbed slowly off the bed, Pete grabbed for the bottle of garlic powder sitting on the bedside table and frantically unscrewed the lid.

The bedroom door swung gently open and Aaron looked in.

"What's going on in here?" Aaron asked. "You boys are supposed to be in bed across the hall."

"Uncle Aaron," Joey whispered. "It's the ghost. He's in the closet."

Aaron stepped inside, but before he could open his mouth, something rustled loudly inside the closet. Startled, he swung toward it and flicked on the overhead light.

Something shot out of the closet—something small, fast, and gray. Pete shrieked and threw the opened bottle of garlic powder in the general direction of the gray streak.

The "ghost" darted across Aaron's feet and out the bedroom door. Startled, Aaron jumped aside. The bottle of garlic powder struck the wall beside him and spread the fragrant spice liberally over his shoulders in a grainy shower.

There was a moment of breathless, thoughtful silence. Felicity stared at the door and at Aaron, then checked surreptitiously to make sure her sleep-shirt hadn't hiked up.

"Nice shot, Pete," Aaron said and looked at Felicity. "Your bedroom and I both smell like chicken cacciatore."

"As I always say, no ghost can abide the presence of garlic in any form." Felicity peered in the direction the "ghost" had fled in an attempt to hide her still-racing heart and shattered nerves.

"Well, Felicity, I see you successfully smoked out the ghost," Aaron said. "I have to admit, you know your stuff."

Felicity collapsed onto the bed and struggled to maintain her cool. "You bet, cowboy. That's what ghost-busters are for, you know."

He wore black pajama bottoms and nothing else. Her mouth went dry just looking at him. His chest was broad and covered with thick, curling hair that called for her touch. For a moment, she wished the two little boys were sleeping soundly across the hall.

Aaron blew garlic powder off his bare arm. The movement made the muscles in his arms move in an utterly fascinating way. "You might try and train your assistant not to throw garlic on the living."

"Sorry. We were somewhat excited at the moment." She lifted her brows. "Are you afraid we might mistake you for a big chuck of chicken cacciatore and take a bite?"

"Felicity said that if any garlic touches the ghost, it'll make him vanish fast," Pete said, panting with residual fright. "And he did, didn't he, Uncle Aaron?"

"I'd say it was the light coming on that made this particular ghost vanish." Aaron came into the room and bent to peer into the depths of the closet. "Let's see what he found so interesting in here."

Felicity stared covetously at his back. It was as tanned and muscular as his front. He bent forward and reached toward the back of the closet, moving aside the suitcases and the shoes.

Aaron turned suddenly. He caught her staring and grinned knowingly. Felicity felt her face heat up. He held up a small paper sack that had a large hole chewed in it. "Well, boys, which one of you is hiding peanuts in the closet?"

There was a moment of silence then Joey spoke up. "They're my peanuts, Uncle Aaron. I forgot where I put them." He moved cautiously to the edge of the bed. "Do ghosts eat peanuts?"

"Ghosts don't, but rats do," Aaron said. "There's nothing a rat likes better than peanuts."

Felicity exhaled and wondered if the weakness in her limbs and the continued rapid flutter of her heartbeat were due to the rat's appearance, or to Aaron's.

"That's what made those weird whispering sounds you kept hearing," she explained to the children. "It was the rat chewing on the peanut shells in order to get to the peanuts inside. The rustling sounds you heard came from the paper sack the peanuts were in."

Joey and Pete regarded the open bag of peanuts with interest. Then they looked at the garlic powder Pete had thrown over the floor and Aaron.

"The garlic powder must have scared off the real ghost," Joey said.

Felicity and Aaron looked at each other, dismayed.

"It wasn't the real ghost," Pete said, to their astonishment. "It's like Uncle Aaron says. We thought the rat was the ghost because it kept making weird noises, and we couldn't see what it was." He stared at the paper sack in Aaron's hands with his small brow wrinkled in deep thought.

"You're right, Pete," Aaron said encouragingly. "When you can't see what's making a strange sound in the middle of the night, it's scary. Turning on a light does a lot to solve the problem."

"Yes," Pete said, and his little face brightened. "Can Joey and I each have our own flashlight, Uncle Aaron? Then we can shine them on the ghost if he bothers us again."

Joey added his voice to Pete's in favor of the flashlights.

"I'll get you both a flashlight first thing tomorrow." Aaron gave Felicity a wry glance. "In the meantime, let's let Felicity go back to bed, and you two had better do the same. Now that this particular ghost has been busted, everyone should be able to sleep well the rest of the night."

"You see?" Felicity asked the room at large. "When you have a competent ghost-buster on the scene, supernatural problems are solved immediately."

Chapter 10

"You don't know how much I appreciate your kindness to my sons," Deborah said at the breakfast table the next morning, as she buttered a piece of cinnamon toast. "Aaron and I have been at such a loss to deal with this ghost idea."

Felicity sipped coffee and gazed out the window at the flat, grassy pastures where Aaron's purebred, red cows grazed peacefully. She wore slim blue jeans with red-fringed boots and a red shirt trimmed with denim that she had chosen with Aaron in mind.

Alas, Aaron had already left for his office, taking Pete and Joey with him. Her own disappointment surprised her. She wondered what he'd look like across the breakfast table from her then told herself she was an idiot for even allowing the thought to cross her mind.

"I think they've decided the ghost is what drove them from their own home." Felicity decided on bluntness. "Their lives were totally disrupted, and the ghost gives them a really good reason for the disruption."

Deborah paled and almost dropped her toast. "Do you think so?"

"Judging from what they told me the day I found them hiding in my closet, yes." Felicity decided she might as well tell Deborah the whole truth whether Aaron liked it or not. "You probably need to sit down with your sons and talk to them about why you've brought them here."

If possible, Deborah turned even paler. "Aaron warned me I needed to be truthful with the boys, but I just can't. Not yet." Her beautiful, blue eyes filled with tears. "It's so hard for me to talk about...about—"

"I'm sure it must be," Felicity soothed. "But you don't have to go into any kind of detail, you know. You can just tell them that you and their father have decided to live apart for a little while."

Deborah dabbed at her eyes with her napkin. Felicity remained silent and slathered butter and strawberry preserves on a slice of toast.

"What makes you think your husband might kidnap the children?" Felicity asked at last.

"He said..." Deborah's voice trailed off, suspended by tears. "He said he was going to come get them and make me come back home if I wanted to be with them."

Felicity frowned. "I think that's just what he meant. He wants you to come back home. If there is a good reason why you can't go back, then you need to tell the boys what it is."

"That's what Aaron says," Deborah choked, trembling visibly. "But he doesn't realize how angry Tony can get, or what he'll do. That's why I'm so afraid he'll kidnap the boys."

After puzzling over these remarks a few moments, and recalling that Polly liked Tony, and so did Aaron, Felicity said, "Well, if he does, at least you'll know where they are. Are you afraid your husband won't take good care of them?"

"Oh, no." Deborah seemed quite positive on this point. "He loves the boys. It's just that I don't want the boys exposed to the other woman in his life. They're too young to understand."

Felicity stared. "The other woman?"

"Yes. He doesn't know I saw him with her, and I've been too upset to confront him about it." Deborah covered her face with her hands. "Aaron doesn't believe it and says I'm probably misinterpreting things."

Felicity blinked. "Aaron likes your husband and probably doesn't want to believe the worst. But you'll have to have it out with Tony sooner or later, especially if he really doesn't know why you left him."

"He says he doesn't know why, but he should," Deborah said. "He was with her at a table for two. In our favorite restaurant," she added, in tones that clinched the matter. "And this was a day after he had yelled at me and stormed out of the house."

"Was he kissing her when you saw them together?"

"It was the next thing to kissing." Tears spilled down Deborah's cheeks. "They were obviously conducting a very intimate conversation."

"You should have gone up to them that very minute," Felicity said. "If anything was going on, you'd know it right away."

"I did know it right away," Deborah insisted. "It was very obvious. No wonder he yelled at me. He's probably tired of me."

Felicity had her doubts about Deborah's interpretation of events, but she knew better than to dwell on the subject any longer. "One thing is certain. If your husband kidnaps the boys, he's the one who will have to deal with the ghost."

Deborah clearly did not find this thought comforting.

"It will be good for him," Felicity said, smiling kindly. "When I was about five, my grandmother kidnapped me. She was mentally ill and had decided to remove me from my mother's evil influence, so she just picked me up one day and drove off with me. She told me Mama was sending me to her house to visit for a while."

"How awful," Deborah said.

Felicity glanced at Deborah. The other woman had forgotten breakfast and sat with her hands tightly clasped, alternately twisting and tugging at the diamond on her left hand.

"Mama never dreamed her own mother had taken me," Felicity said. "I knew my grandmother was peculiar, but I was used to obeying lots of different relatives because my mother was on the road so much."

"Oh, God," Deborah whispered, anguished. "How awful for your poor mother."

Felicity agreed. "There were no clues and no ransom demands, and after six weeks, the authorities told her I was probably dead. The general opinion was that I'd been snatched from our own apartment and killed."

"Your poor mother," Deborah whispered, dead white.

Felicity could only guess at how terrible that time had been for her mother. That was the real reason she never demurred at how many times a day Becky called her. Becky needed the security of hearing her daughter's voice.

"I didn't know I'd been kidnapped until one night I saw my mother crying on television," Felicity went on. "When my grandmother wouldn't let me call and comfort her, I realized suddenly that she'd been lying to me. So I left in order to find a telephone."

"You're so brave," Deborah said. "I could never do such a thing."

"My great escape didn't require a lot of daring," Felicity said drily. "My grandmother had locked me in the bathroom, so I crawled out the window and shimmied up the vent stack to the roof. I climbed down a tree on the other side of her house."

"You must have been a very clever child." Deborah clearly considered her some sort of child-Houdini. "Most children would never think of defying an adult that way."

"I was really upset to see my mother crying," Felicity said. "All I could think of was calling to tell her I was all right. A policeman picked me up when he saw me walking down the street in the middle of the night."

Deborah took a shaky sip of coffee. "What wonderful news for your poor mother."

Felicity remembered the dead silence that had greeted her young ears when she'd managed to phone Becky at last. Becky had fainted for the first and only time in her life.

"Poor Mama thought she was talking to my ghost."

The unfortunate mention of the word *ghost* made Deborah wince. "I was wondering…" she said hesitantly.

"Yes?"

"What would you do if you thought your husband was seeing another woman?"

Felicity pressed her lips together before she could say she would likely take some sort of physical action. After a moment of thought, she spoke.

"First, I'd try to catch them together. Once I had them both together, I'd walk up and confront them, just in case I was wrong. There could be an innocent explanation, you know."

Two big tears rolled down Deborah's pale cheeks. "What if Tony is bored with me? All the women he meets at work are so interesting, so much more…" Her voice trailed off.

"Then it's time to take some action to become more interesting." Felicity reached across the table and patted Deborah's hand. "Have you talked to your husband since you left him?"

Deborah shook her head, blinded by tears. "I just don't know what to say to him. He keeps calling, but I hang up or let Polly answer."

"You haven't told him why you left?"

"Oh, no. How could I?"

Felicity had to close her mouth forcibly a second time. "How could you not? I mean if he's really seeing another woman, he deserves to know the consequences of his actions, don't you think?"

Deborah buried her face in her napkin. "I'm afraid of him. He—he can get me to do anything."

Felicity decided Tony Sachitano must be a man even bigger and tougher-looking than Aaron. Deborah seemed so fragile, the man probably terrified the life out of her.

"He—he's so strong, and so *volatile*," Deborah went on. "If he…were to get angry, I couldn't stand it. I can't bear any more, Felicity. I just can't." Deborah dissolved into tears and added, between sobs, "And I've got to get a job so I can support my children, and I just don't know what to do. I've never worked before."

Felicity bit her lip.

"Aaron never wanted me to work while I was in school," Deborah said. "He thought it would harm my health and affect my grades." She sighed and added, "Our mother died when I was ten, and our father was an alcoholic, so for all practical purposes, Aaron served as my parent. He was older and very responsible…" She trailed off and added, "I had awful asthma as a child, and Aaron was afraid I might die before I could grow up."

Studying the air of mental and physical frailty Deborah projected, Felicity acquitted Aaron of over-protecting his sister. Anyone would have done the same.

"If you have to get a job, I'm sure you'll find something you'll enjoy," she said. "Besides, it may not come to that. Maybe Aaron can talk to Tony."

Deborah looked doubtful. "Tony is…Tony is…I just don't want Aaron to get hurt because of this."

Felicity studied her plate in startled silence. Not many men were likely to be bigger or tougher than Aaron. How dangerous *was* Tony Sachitano? Maybe she ought to find out.

Accordingly, she returned to her own house and spent the larger part of the day plowing through more trash and stuffing it into large garbage bags, which she stowed on the front porch until she could find out where or how to dispose of household trash. The front porch now hosted a goodly pile of the sacks, and the living room had achieved a reasonably uncluttered look at last.

Well-pleased with her efforts, Felicity turned her thoughts toward the problem of Tony Sachitano. When she spotted Aaron's pickup truck in the driveway next door and saw the two little boys racing toward the barn, she walked over and found them in the stalls, diligently brushing their two ponies. They confirmed her worst fears.

Pete said with enthusiasm, "My daddy is the biggest man in the whole world."

"Bigger than your Uncle Aaron?" Felicity jumped nervously when Rhyolite snorted at her from the adjoining stall.

"Our daddy is *big*," Joey added. "Really big—and strong."

That settled it, as far as Felicity was concerned. Tony Sachitano had probably made his way through college by playing tackle for the University of Texas or something. She leaned against the stall door and thought on the matter.

"You may as well pet Rhyolite," Aaron said from behind her. "He took a liking to you the day you rode him."

Felicity edged away. "He's probably wondering what I taste like. If you've got a minute, I'd like to talk to you."

"Now, Miss Clayton, horses are vegetarians." Aaron blocked her retreat, smiling encouragingly. "Come on in and let me show you how to pet a horse. Then we can talk."

"Thanks, but no thanks. I've got to get back to sorting through junk. The living room is finally somewhat clean, so I'll be starting on the kitchen next."

"You're bound to be worn out, what with all the ghost-busting last night." He took her arm and guided her gently toward the stall. "This won't take but a minute."

"I need to check in at my shop. It's time for our biannual inventory—"

Thanks to her confusion at Aaron's nearness, Felicity didn't realize what was happening until he opened a stall door and propelled her inside. She dug her red-fringed boots into the concrete too late.

She tried to edge around him. "I'm supposed to meet the real estate agent this afternoon. I really don't have time for this."

Aaron didn't seem to hear her. "Easy, boy. I've brought you an old friend who's been avoiding you lately."

"Who says?" Felicity quavered. "Will you stop shoving?"

"Reach out with your right hand and stroke his forehead," Aaron said.

"Who, me? No, thank you."

"Cowgirl, you have an image to uphold. The horse is waiting. Take your time."

Felicity stared, frozen, at Rhyolite, who eyed her back in an interested way. She could have sworn the horse was curious to see what she was going to do next.

Rhyolite snorted and blew gently from wide, flexible nostrils. She gasped and stepped back into Aaron's broad chest. He imitated a brick wall in immovability.

"Go ahead," Aaron said softly. He slid his arms around her waist. "He's wondering why you aren't touching him. You wouldn't want to hurt his feelings, would you?"

"He has feelings?"

"Put out your right hand and stroke his head."

"I'll tell you a secret. I'm a saleswoman, not a cowgirl."

"You're a true cowgirl at heart. Trust me."

She knew she was being ridiculous, but stretching out her hand to pet the big horse was a tough proposition. Felicity took a deep breath, held it, and stretched out her hand. Nothing happened. Rhyolite watched, and so did Felicity, as her hand came within six inches of his muzzle and stopped.

Rhyolite shoved his soft, gray muzzle into her hand. Felicity shook, but she couldn't jump backward because of Aaron. Forced to stand her ground, she gathered her courage and stroked her hand gently over the horse's forehead.

"Now give him these." Aaron placed several sugar cubes in her hand.

She held out her hand, palm flat. There was nothing to this horse business after all. One just had to have courage. Her courage left in a gasp when the horse lipped the cubes from her palm. She remained frozen in position, palm out, until Aaron gently pulled her arm back.

"Rhyolite is now your slave," Aaron guided her out and shut the stall door. "He'll make sure you get an extra-smooth ride next time you take him out."

That would be never. Felicity said nothing and led the way out of the stable, setting a swift pace. Aaron probably thought she was a first-class coward, but she didn't care at the moment.

Aaron laughed and caught up to her. "Slow down. What was it you wanted to talk to me about?"

She glanced around. Pete and Joey were still occupied inside the stables, grooming their ponies. "Do you think Tony Sachitano really is going to come here?"

He led her to the fence that enclosed the pasture where he let his saddle horses run and leaned against it. Felicity laid both her palms on the top rail and gazed absently at Quiche. Aaron slipped an arm across her shoulders in the way she had seen him do with Deborah and drew her close to his side. He stood beside her in silence for a moment.

"I'm surprised he hasn't come," he said at last. "That's what had me worried—the fact that he hasn't come yet."

"You're worried because he *hasn't* come?"

"That's right. Tony's a great guy. I've always liked him, and he's always treated Deborah with kid gloves, just the way she needed. So I'm at a loss as to what's gone wrong, and all Deb will say is that he's seeing another woman. Frankly, I find it hard to believe, but nothing will be sorted out until he does come."

Felicity fell silent. Obviously, Aaron had the typical male outlook. Maybe he didn't realize he was now the official protector of the woman Tony Sachitano had claimed as his own. That made him the automatic target of Tony's wrath.

"This is one trouble I can't pull Deborah out of," Aaron said, in a soft rumble. "If I thought Tony was beating her or the children, I'd probably kill him, but she assures me it's nothing like that. Deb is going to have to handle this on her own."

She turned to stare at him. "Don't you think you should be a little worried about this?"

"This, from you?" Aaron's smile went crooked. "You're the one who's made me see that I've been guilty of fighting so many of Deb's battles for her, she hasn't learned any fighting skills of her own. I'm here for her if she needs me, but I'm refusing to get involved in whatever her quarrel is with her husband. It's strictly between the two of them. As far as I'm concerned, the sooner she goes face to face with Tony, the better." He sighed and added, "What worries me is why he hasn't come before now."

Felicity felt frozen with astonishment. Aaron was taking lessons in family relationships from *her*?

He touched her chin gently with one big finger. "Don't look so shocked. You've been good for us. For me, especially. You're a real cowgirl—a woman of true courage."

She looked at him in blank surprise but made no protest when he gathered her into his arms and stood holding her. The feel of his big, strong body against hers made her rest her head on his shoulder and slide her arms around his waist. Reminding herself that she ought to head back to those junked-up kitchen cabinets did nothing to ease the urge to run her hands over his shoulders and smooth her fingers over his back muscles.

Felicity stared into Aaron's dark blue eyes and was lost. He cupped her jaw with both his hands and brought his lips to hers slowly, slowly. By the time he made contact with her mouth, Felicity quivered with anticipation. She flung her arms around his neck and hugged him hard against her, glorying in the hard strength of his body.

Aaron groaned aloud and locked her against him while he kissed her with a desire that threatened to burst the bounds she had set. In fact, Felicity feared that if a bed or a fluffy haystack had been within sight, she might have tumbled him down and had her way with him.

"Ssshhhh," Pete said. "Uncle Aaron's kissing Felicity."

"Why?" Joey asked.

"I dunno. It's just something grown-ups do. It means they like each other."

"Then why doesn't Felicity kiss us?" Joey asked, injured.

Felicity tried to push Aaron away, but he held her against him, chuckling softly.

"Felicity does kiss you," he said.

"Not like that," Joey asserted.

"That's because it's a kind of kissing only grown-ups do," Aaron explained. "You're both still a little short yet."

Felicity tried to pretend her face didn't resemble a fresh radish. If she was lucky, the boys would forget all about this little interlude in another few hours.

On the other hand, when had she ever been lucky?

Joey considered the matter a moment. "Come on, Pete. Let's go get the stool in the kitchen to stand on so Felicity can kiss us."

"Sorry, boys," Aaron said, grinning. He locked Felicity against him. "I saw her first."

• • •

Aaron managed to get Felicity to agree to eat dinner with them, although she insisted on heading back to her own home so she could make a start on cleaning out the kitchen cabinets. Altogether, he was not displeased with her reaction to him, and he intended to take his courtship to the next level just as soon as he could get her alone. Given that the boys considered her their special property, he figured he'd have to take her back to her own home before he could be alone with her.

His instincts proved correct. Pete and Joey appropriated Felicity the moment she arrived for dinner. She wore a long, slim black denim skirt with those ridiculous red-fringed black cowboy boots and a red western shirt with coral and silver cufflinks. With it, she wore a silver, Native American necklace inlaid with red coral and dangling earrings of silver strands tipped with beads of red coral. Although he couldn't have described one single item of her outfit, he admitted the overall effect was one of eye-catching high fashion.

"Come on in, honey," Aaron said. Pete had one of her hands and Joey tugged at the other. "Ordinarily, we're more calm around here, but we've had an exciting evening."

"My daddy called," Joey said. "He's coming to see us."

"Next weekend," Pete added. "He's going to talk to Uncle Aaron about bringing our ponies to Fort Worth. We can put them in our garage and buy them some hay."

"Don't forget the oats," Felicity said. "That's wonderful news, Joey. I'm so glad to hear that."

She gave Aaron a questioning look and he shook his head. No need to tell her that Deborah had taken to her bed with a wet cloth on her forehead, and that she had continued refusing to talk to her husband. She claimed she had nothing to say to him.

"He's coming next weekend," Joey said. "How soon is that, Uncle Aaron?"

"It's eight days from now," Aaron specified. "Don't worry, Joey. I'll make sure you're ready to meet him."

Both Joey and Pete appeared satisfied by this, although their excitement remained unabated. They chattered all through the excellent supper of beef stew and vegetables about how they would fix their garage up for their ponies. After Polly had served them dishes of ice cream and apple pie, they put their heads together over a sheet of drawing paper and plotted out just where in the garage they intended to build each pony a stall.

Felicity looked at Aaron with a smile and lifted her brows. "It's quite an engineering feat to turn a garage into a stable. I'll bet they sleep really well tonight."

"I'm counting on it." He understood her unspoken intent. "All else has been forgotten in the excitement. If Deb can manage to pull herself together over the next few days, any otherworldly visitors will be long forgotten."

"Maybe she'd like to come help me turn out the dining room and kitchen." Felicity spooned up ice cream in a way that riveted his attention. "Now that I've gotten the living room fairly cleaned out, I'm no longer afraid to let anyone walk into the house."

"You've got quite a pile of plastic bags on the porch." Aaron watched her full lips close around the spoon and was rewarded with a glimpse of the silver bands on her teeth. "Maybe you'd like me to haul them to the dump for you."

"I have a truck scheduled to arrive in two more days," Felicity said. "That's why I could use some extra help. He's going to haul off most of the furniture, along with all the bags of trash."

"We'll all help." He watched with fascination as she forked up a bite of apple pie. "In fact, I'll walk you back home after supper. We'll get those kitchen cabinets done tonight."

He tried not to think about what he'd like to do with her in the bedroom. Otherwise, he was likely to rush her straight to the bed without even a pause in the kitchen. To his gratification, Felicity looked at him as though she might like to be rushed straight back to her bedroom.

"Thanks, cowboy," she said. "That would be such a big help, I can't even tell you."

"No sign yet of your mother's songs?"

"Nothing." Felicity frowned over her next forkful of Polly's excellent apple pie. "What's worse is that before I can even have all that old furniture hauled off, I'll have to check each piece over for hidden compartments and hollow legs. There's no telling where Grandma Lureen could have hidden those songs, as paranoid as she was."

"Don't worry. We'll go over everything and chop into it with an ax if we have to." Didn't she know he would do anything he could to help her? "She didn't have a safety deposit box or a storage room anywhere, did she?"

"If she did, she probably forgot about it and let the payments lapse." Felicity bit her lip. "I'm hoping that's not what happened, but who knows? Mama thinks those songs are gone forever, but I can't help feeling they're hidden somewhere in that house, in the middle of all that junk."

"If they are, we'll find them," Aaron promised, vowing to scour the house from top to bottom himself, if that was what it took.

After supper, he and Felicity sat in the living room with cups of coffee and listened while Pete and Joey each explained in detail just how they intended to care for their ponies when they got stalls built into their Fort Worth garage.

Deborah, as he had expected, did not appear, but he hoped that by tomorrow morning, she might have gotten her courage back. Every time he had urged her to face Tony and have it out with him, she had moaned that she just couldn't talk to him yet, and buried her face again in a white tissue.

At eight o'clock, he sent the little boys to bed, pleased when they made no protest. It was as if the ghost Felicity had exorcised the night before had never existed, although they did beg Felicity to come help Aaron turn out their bedroom light for the night.

At last he had the two children in their beds. His breath quickened with anticipation as he escorted Felicity out the front door and shut it carefully behind him.

"Well, Miss Clayton," he said softly. "I have to admit, you do good work. That ghost is now out of sight and out of mind."

"It'll stay that way if their dad makes it here to see them," she agreed. "Do you think your sister is going to be all right with that?"

Aaron grinned with wry humor. "I'm afraid not, but there's not a lot she can do about it unless she wants to get a job and move into her own place. I've told her she doesn't have any right to keep Tony from seeing the boys, and that as long as they're under this roof, they're completely safe."

Felicity walked beside him in the dark, glancing up at the starlit skies in appreciation. "I don't understand why she hasn't confronted him yet if she really believes he's seeing another woman."

"Neither can I, but Deb—" He shrugged. "Our father was an alcoholic, very volatile, and scary to someone like Deb. After he died, I did what I could, but no doubt about it, that affected her. Tony may have gotten angry and said a few things he shouldn't have said." He shrugged and watched her profile, dimly visible against the distant porch light that glowed from her house. "From everything Tony says, it sounds as if he has no idea what caused all this. I'm staying strictly out of it. Deb is going to have to handle this on her own."

"I think you're right." Felicity quickened her pace, staring towards her front porch. "Something's happened to all my trash bags."

"What?"

Aaron studied the porch, dimly visible in the yellowish glow of the porch light Felicity had left burning. As they drew nearer, he realized the trash bags had been slashed open and scattered all over the porch.

"Hold up, honey," he said, narrowing his eyes against the gloom. "Looks like your front door is standing open. You'd better stop right here."

Felicity gasped. "Someone's in my house."

She sounded so outraged, Aaron grabbed her arm. "Forget it. You call the sheriff while I go check things out. Whoever it is may still be in there."

As he expected, Felicity followed him almost to the front porch, stopping only when he turned and forcibly blocked her. He waited while she pulled her cell phone out of her pocket and pecked in the Foxe emergency number then he walked slowly toward the front steps, peering inside the front door.

He saw no sign of anyone, but he did note that the front door had been kicked open. A big scrape decorated the center panel, as if someone's boot heel had scuffed it, and Felicity's brand-new lock gleamed amidst splinters of wood where the door had been shattered.

Inside was even more chaotic. The neat living room had been reduced to rubble. The old sofa had been slashed open so that its stuffing protruded, and the chairs and coffee table were upended and broken.

Felicity stared inside, looking shocked while she spoke to the sheriff's office, but she made no move to come inside. Aaron motioned for her to stay put.

The kitchen cabinets had been thrown open and their contents emptied onto the floor. Aaron glanced in and saw that even the drawers had been pulled out and upended.

Every room of the small house had been trashed, he realized, as if whoever had done it clearly intended to send Felicity a message. He moved cautiously toward her bedroom and pushed open the half-closed door.

The message was very clear, and it had been hand-printed on a sheet of paper that lay on the bedspread.

Call off the dogs, it read, in huge block letters.

Chapter 11

Felicity did not argue when Aaron emerged from checking through the house and told her she was either coming home with him or he was staying with her. She waited with him on the front porch until the sheriff and one of his deputies arrived to photograph the mess and take down information.

"Thank goodness he didn't trash my bedroom or slash up my clothes," Felicity said as she packed up her suitcase. "I'd have really been upset." She glanced around the untouched room. "I wonder why he didn't."

"Probably because he wants to scare you a little, not infuriate you." Aaron grinned, watching her reach carefully into the closet and lift out several fringed, colorful blouses. "I'd say this guy is playing things very carefully. He wants you concerned enough to take action, but not so concerned, you'll sic even more 'dogs' on him."

"Mama being the biggest 'dog,' I suppose," Felicity said, sounding resigned. "She's still hot on his trail. The last word she had is that he was hiding out in Arkansas."

"I'd say he's in Texas now." Aaron stood in the door and watched as she hung the garments back in the closet. "That means you'd better have someone with you every time you go anywhere in town."

"Are you volunteering, cowboy?" she asked, tossing him a sidelong glance.

"You'd better believe it. I'd like nothing better than to get my hands on this guy." Aaron looked pointedly around at the destruction.

149

"If you'll notice, he hadn't hurt anything that I didn't intend to get rid of in the first place," she observed. "In fact, it's odd the way he carefully avoided my bedroom. I really, really expected to find all my clothes slashed into ribbons, but he didn't touch anything in here."

"Don't start feeling sorry for the guy," Aaron said, scowling. "He's still dangerous. The fact that he'd threaten you says it all as far as I'm concerned."

"Don't worry. I'm still mad at him for undoing all the careful work I've done these past few days." Assuming it was Gary Carlisle, he'd emptied several of the trash bags from the front porch over the floors around the house. The rest had been slashed open to shed their contents throughout the surrounding pastureland. "I'll re-bag the trash and pack the bags into my truck bed tonight. I'm afraid trash will be all over the landscape if I wait until tomorrow."

Aaron followed Felicity into the living room and reached down to right the old sofa. "Sit down a minute, honey. I'll see if I can find some more trash bags."

"There's a box lying on the floor by the cabinets." She sat down carefully in her slim, black skirt, avoiding the yellowish cotton stuffing poking through the slashes.

Aaron righted the coffee table and sat down beside her, propping his boot heels on the table. He combed his fingers through his hair and caught her gaze upon him. "Are you all right?"

Felicity sighed again. "Sure. It's just such a nuisance to have somebody deliberately undo all that work, even though it looks like there's no real harm done."

He leaned back and rested his arm along the back of the sofa behind her. "Come on, honey. Cheer up. If you're worried about the mess, I'm going to help you."

Felicity looked at the mess and winced. "Thank you. Tomorrow I'll start taking apart all this old furniture and getting rid of it. Then I'll rent some furniture so Mama can stay with me during the Rice Festival. She says she's looking forward to sleeping in a real bed for a change."

The kitchen telephone rang before Aaron could reply.

"You'd better get that," Aaron said. "It's bound to be your mother."

Felicity rose automatically. "I don't know why she'd call that phone when she knows I've got my cell."

"Why are you here?" Becky demanded. "I thought you were going over to eat supper at Aaron's house."

"Hello, Mama. I did, and he just walked me back."

"Tell her about Carlisle," Aaron ordered from the sofa. If he knew Felicity, she had no intentions of worrying her mother by mentioning the night's events.

Felicity shook her head violently, as he expected.

"What did he say?" Becky asked. "Did I hear him mention that nasty ol' Gary Carlisle?"

Felicity glanced toward the living room and directed an exaggerated frown at Aaron. "Yes, Mama. I told him the story, and he's with you on that subject."

"Tell her what happened tonight," Aaron said loudly.

Felicity slapped her hand over the receiver mouthpiece. "Hush up, Aaron. We don't need her flying down here."

He could hear Becky's annoyed exclamations from where he was. "If you don't tell her, I will."

"Oh, all right." Exasperated, Felicity scowled at him and turned her back. "Calm down, Mama. It's just that someone broke in and trashed the house tonight while I was next door eating supper with Aaron and his family. Nothing was damaged, but—"

At once, Aaron heard Becky erupt. He smothered his grin.

"Now, Mama, Aaron is with me, and he's already searched the house. Everything is fine, and the sheriff says so, too. But I'm going to go back to Aaron's house and spend the night there." She paused and listened a moment. "No, Mama, I don't know why anyone would trash this place. There's nothing worth stealing here except my clothes, but—"

"Unless it was that Carlisle fellow," Aaron nearly shouted.

Felicity held the phone out to Aaron. "She wants to talk to you."

Aaron took the phone and informed Becky in succinct terms of what had happened and what he suspected while watching Felicity wander about the room uprighting chairs.

He finished with, "Felicity thinks all he wants is for you to stop your pursuit and drop the charges against him. Otherwise, she thinks he would have shredded her clothes and done some real damage."

There was a silence while Becky assimilated the information. "What do you think, Aaron?" she asked at last. "Should I let him get away with hurtin' my baby the way he did?"

Aaron gave a grim chuckle and watched Felicity kneel to pick up and thumb through books that were scattered across the floor from a small, overturned bookcase. "Felicity thinks he's been punished enough, but if you want to know what I think, there's no punishment harsh enough for the kind of screwball who'd pull something like what he pulled."

"My sentiments exactly," Becky said with considerable satisfaction. "There ain't no bribe big enough to get me off his case."

"Aaron," Felicity shrieked suddenly. She knelt before the overturned bookcase, staring at something on the bottom of it.

"What's happened?" Becky yelled.

He held the phone away from his ear. "What is it? I don't—Say, what is that?"

Felicity pointed to the exposed bottom shelf of the bookcase, where an old manila envelope had been fastened with silver duct tape. "It could be Mama's songs. But don't say anything to her.

Let me look first." She reached for a strip of the duct tape with trembling hands and gently worked it away from the envelope.

"What is it?" Becky demanded. "What's happening?"

"Hold on a minute," Aaron said. "There's no danger, but Felicity thinks she's found something. Give us a minute while we look to see what it is."

Becky subsided, although Aaron sensed the rising motherly anxiety on the other end of the wire. He laid the receiver on the kitchen counter and went to kneel beside Felicity. He used his pocket knife to detach the envelope from the layers of ancient duct tape that secured it to the underside of the small book case. Slitting the envelope open carefully, he pulled out a stack of yellowed paper covered with bold, dark pencil script and musical notations and held them before Felicity's wide gaze.

"Go speak to your mother, honey. Ask her if one of her songs was called 'The Outcome of Our Love.'"

Felicity's eyes had filled with tears, but she obeyed him with alacrity, barely able to choke out the question. She held the receiver away from her ear when it gave vent to a loud shriek and closed her eyes as two big tears rolled down her cheeks.

"That's them," Becky yelled. "Praise the Lord."

Aaron could hear the words clearly from across the room. He laughed exultantly and held the songs out to Felicity. The sight of her tears tore at his heart.

He reached for her. "Now, honey, don't cry."

"I can't help it." Felicity let him hold her, clutching the telephone receiver to her ear. "You have no idea what this means to Mama. She wants to thank you for your part in helping find them."

Aaron took the receiver she held out to him. To his discomfort, Becky was crying, too. In the way of great artists, she fully experienced her emotional release by crying out loud and with great zest.

He listened to Becky's loud sobbing a moment and passed the phone back to Felicity. "I think she'd rather talk to you."

• • •

Felicity barely noticed when Aaron helped her into his truck. Dazed, she peered through the darkness at the house and cradled Becky's precious songs in her arms. Now that she had actually found the songs, she could call in professionals to clean the house and trash all the furniture.

Aaron obligingly drove her to a print shop that acted as a pickup point for Federal Express and waited while she photocopied each song, then addressed a mailer to the address of Becky's next stop.

"Now, sugar, don't worry," he said, as if reading her mind. "Federal Express doesn't lose things. That package will reach your mother's hands by tomorrow afternoon."

Felicity nodded, biting her lip and squeezing back tears. "I've made two sets of copies, just in case it doesn't." She smiled at him gratefully. "We can probably expect a new album soon that'll be different from anything she's ever done before."

"She wrote those songs while your father was still alive, didn't she?" Aaron asked. "Do you think he knew about them?"

Felicity turned the mailer over to the clerk and paid the fee. Aaron's rough, gentle voice played on every nerve ending she had, plus a few new ones. "That's the only thing she's held on to all these years. She says she sang every one of them to him before he was killed."

Aaron touched her arm gently. "She must have loved him a lot."

"She did. He was her world."

Felicity stared at Aaron's sun-darkened hand with its calloused palms and fingers. When he touched her, she felt almost as if she'd been jolted by several hundred volts of electricity. She opened her mouth to tell him she wanted to go to a motel rather than back to his house. Something told her it would be far safer for her peace of mind.

"Come on, honey," Aaron said. "If your mouth is still open when we get back outside, you'll wind up swallowing love bugs."

Felicity closed her mouth. "Love bugs?"

"They're the little black bugs plastered all over the front of your truck. You'd better get them off pretty soon or they'll ruin the finish."

"Oh." The collection of small, black insects on her truck grill and windshield was growing steadily thicker. She hadn't yet had time to find a car wash.

"The place down the street has some new carwash liquid in," the clerk offered, returning Felicity's change. "It's guaranteed to get love bugs off your paint job."

"I'll keep it in mind." Felicity followed Aaron out the door. "I know I'll be sorry for asking, but why do you call them love bugs?"

Aaron lifted his hand and closed it around one of the black forms floating in the air. He held it before her face and opened it to show the black bug centered on his palm. "Take a look."

She looked and saw that the little black bug wasn't one insect but two. "Oh."

Aaron let the bugs go, chuckling. "When they're flying, any moving vehicle is soon plastered with them, and they're hell to get off."

She tried not to dwell on the thoughts of lovemaking the bugs conjured up. "Is that right?" She felt like an idiot, blushing like this, and Aaron was obviously enjoying her discomfiture.

"Stop blushing, honey. You look like a virgin."

Little did he know. "I'm not blushing. I'm cooling off my core."

"I affect you that strongly?" He was laughing as he opened his truck door and helped her step inside. "Someday very soon I am going to affect you just that way."

Felicity gulped back a reply. She could say nothing without sounding like a blushing virgin. God forbid Aaron should learn that was exactly what she was, and that he already affected her more powerfully than any other man ever had.

"In fact," Aaron continued provocatively, "by this time next week, you'll be blushing every time I smile at you."

"A week?" Felicity's head whirled. "My, you cowboys sure do work fast, don't you? Are you planning to walk past me in your G-string or something?"

"Or something," Aaron said, grinning. "Must be the love bugs."

Felicity sucked in her breath. Maybe it was the love bugs. Who knew? But it did not matter at all to her, because Aaron was the man she wanted for her first lover, and the sooner, the better.

So how did one go about propositioning a man? She ran a few trite phrases through her mind and rejected them one by one while Aaron drove them back to his home.

"Let's go back to my house," she said, as a preliminary. "I don't think Gary will bother me anymore, now that he's delivered his message."

Aaron was silent while he turned his truck in her driveway. "You do realize, I hope, that I can't leave you alone in this house, with no lock on the door." It was a statement rather than a question.

Felicity smiled inwardly and said, "We'll talk about it inside."

He parked the truck and came around to help her down. "There's plenty of room at my place. You wouldn't be in the way at all."

"I can see that." She stood in the circle of his arms and gazed up at him in the dim, yellowish light cast by the front porch light. "Ranching those red cows of yours must be a mighty lucrative business."

"Selling trucks and cars is what keeps the bills paid, honey." Aaron smiled. "Those Brahmins keep the pastures in good shape and give my horses some useful work to do." He ran his hands down her arms and pulled her flush against his body. "What I need is a woman who can do the same for me."

"Oh, I have lots of useful work you can do," Felicity said, surprising herself. "In fact, there's something really useful you can do for me tonight."

Aaron drew in his breath as if he didn't trust her meaning. "Since I've already bagged the trash and straightened the furniture, am I allowed to hope this useful work involves you and a comfortable bed?"

"They do say visualization makes things happen the way you want them to." She hoped he heard the sincerity in her voice. "The sooner you begin the better, as far as I'm concerned."

His hands, flattened on her back, trembled slightly. "You took the words right out of my mouth. Come on in, cowgirl. Let's see if we can make a start on all this work."

Felicity shivered with anticipation and hurried inside. The lights, which they had left on, were way too bright for what she had in mind, so she turned off every one of them except a small lamp beside the old sofa. Aaron stacked a couple of chairs against the broken door.

He walked her to her bedroom and stepped back reluctantly. "I'd better check the other rooms, just in case. Stay right here, honey."

Felicity was so far gone, she almost told him to forget the house. She stood in the center of the bedroom, temporarily at a loss, and wondered what to do next.

Whatever comes naturally, ran the words of one of Becky's songs, in answer to that very question. This was not a good time to discover she had no idea what ought to come naturally. Fortunately, Aaron knew what to do next and how to go about it. He returned a moment later, locked the bedroom door behind him and turned to stare at her.

Felicity melted. Something about the hungry look on his face spoke to her deepest instincts. Moving slowly, with great deliberation, she unfastened her silver cufflinks and laid them on the dresser. Next off was the coral and turquoise necklace. For a moment she regretted all the different articles she had to remove, one at a time, in order to perform a proper striptease, until she saw Aaron's face. Then she wished she had worn a few more items that needed removing. His appreciation spurred her on. He remained by the door, watching her every move in a silence fraught with tension.

She removed the silver rosette belt she wore and laid it on the dresser then took the silver wires out of her ears. The coral bits clicked together in a gentle tinkling as she laid them beside the matching necklace. Then she removed her two coral and turquoise rings and placed them beside her earrings, and sat down on the bed to remove her red-fringed black boots.

She began on the buttons of her blouse, gently working each one loose, until the entire blouse was unbuttoned. She unsnapped the catch of her long, black denim skirt and stepped out of it. Carefully she draped both items over the dresser chair and stood before him wearing only a chemise and long half-slip.

He remained standing beside the door with both feet firmly planted, watching her every move with narrowed, hungry eyes. For a moment, she wished he would take command and remove the rest of her clothing himself, until she realized he was allowing her to control the encounter. Warmth washed through her and she was no longer afraid. Perhaps she had been misinformed about women's first experiences with men.

She slipped off the rest of her clothes then turned to look at Aaron. He came to her immediately and took her in his arms, molding her body against his.

"You're like quicksilver," he said in his gravelly voice. "Sleek and changeable and sexy as hell." He stared at her mouth. "Like

I said, you don't need jewelry. Those braces look like jewelry on you."

She felt sexy when he looked at her like that, his eyes dark with passion. She looped her arms around his neck and leaned into him, glorying in the feel of his lean, hard body against her smooth curves.

His rough hands smoothed over her arms and back while he kissed her and traced his tongue over her braces before dipping deeper. Then he cupped her bottom and moved against her to let her know, without question, how much he wanted her.

Felicity trembled and melted further. In another moment, she would be a molten pool of desire at his feet. Before she could warn him of that fact, he lifted her and carried her to the bed. He bent and swept the covers down in one smooth motion and laid her gently in the center.

He straightened, still staring at her with that hungry navy-blue stare, and stripped off his own clothing in a graceless, hasty way that nevertheless enchanted her. He wanted her, and he wanted her to know it.

When he returned to her, he was totally naked, and she found him beautiful. Dimly she wondered when she should feel nervous then decided it didn't matter. How could a woman feel nervous when she had a man like this to look forward to?

The thought passed briefly through her mind that perhaps she ought to warn him that she was inexperienced, but she banished it as quickly as it surfaced. The last thing she wanted was to slow down his possession of her, and something told her that this piece of information would definitely call a halt to the proceedings.

He kissed her breasts and drew them into his mouth, one at a time. His slow, deliberate attentions to each nipple almost sent her over the edge of sanity.

She poured herself over him like liquid mercury, savoring the feel of his chest and powerful arms. In her pliable state, she likened him to pure, hardened steel and welcomed him into her body.

To her joy, he wasted no more time. Locking her mouth against his, he smothered her swift exclamation of shock when he penetrated her and gave her a few seconds to adjust to his size and weight. Felicity professed herself amazed at just how fast she adapted to fit him. They might have been made for each other. In fact, the more she thought about it, the more certain she grew that Aaron had been created especially for her.

She had never experienced anything like this, she admitted to herself, and it had been well worth the wait. Something told her that no other man of her acquaintance, and certainly not poor old Gary Carlisle, could have made her feel the way she felt in Aaron's arms.

The intimate storm of feeling he created inside her kept on building and building, until she wondered how she could possibly contain it without exploding. Then she did explode, into a kaleidoscope of stars and colors that left her panting and trembling all over as the euphoria flooded every cell of her body, from her head to the tips of her toes.

Aaron appeared to find the experience as earthshaking as she did, much to her delight. He groaned, a harsh sound of complete pleasure, and stilled, breathing hard. He remained where he was for a moment, staring down at her with his intense, navy gaze, then slowly moved to lie beside her.

He said nothing until his breathing had steadied, which was fine with Felicity. She pillowed her head on his shoulder and gazed at what she could see of his chest. She might never move again.

"You should have told me," he said, when he could speak.

"Told you what?" she purred and moved her hand gently across the broad expanse of chest before her eyes.

"That you've never been with a man before." He reached over to touch her chin and make her look at him. "Did you think I wouldn't notice?"

Felicity shrugged as well as she could, considering her position. "What does it matter? There's a first time for everyone, you know. It's not something you broadcast around these days."

Aaron regarded her with a solemn expression that enchanted her with its intensity. "Did I hurt you?"

"Do I look hurt?"

"No, but—"

"I'm not a brilliant actress, so believe me, if I felt hurt, you'd know all about it in no short order." She smiled at him suggestively. "I'm happy to report that I feel great. Better than great, in fact. And you, Aaron Whitaker, are in a position to make me feel even better."

"I am?" He regarded her with a hopeful smile.

"That's right." She stretched out one hand in a languid way that emphasized her current state of total relaxation. "You can start again at the very beginning and repeat every move you just made, because it was absolutely perfect."

"That kind of talk will get you anything you want," Aaron said.

"Anything?"

"Anything," he repeated, and proceeded to prove it.

• • •

Aaron awakened as dawn began to lighten the sky and remained still so he could enjoy the feel of Felicity's soft breath against his neck. Her soft weight lay on his arm, and the curve of her hip pressed against his side. For a woman who was new to lovemaking, she seemed to know all the right moves.

But she lived in Nashville, and she intended to return there within—he checked his mental calendar—a little more than a week, right after her mother's appearance at the Rice Festival. That meant he had about a week to show her what a man could do to make a woman happy.

He smiled wryly into the semi-darkness. Somewhere along the line he had developed a fierce desire to coax her into moving her base of operations from Nashville to Foxe, and more particularly, into his home and life. Judging from the free-ranging life she had led up until the past year or two that might not be easy. But he had a lot of dedication, and few things that were really worthwhile were easy.

He began his campaign that afternoon, when Felicity walked over to join him and his two nephews in the big barn.

"I thought we'd start your riding lessons this morning with a short trip around the pastures," he said.

"My what?" Felicity looked startled and not particularly thrilled.

"Oh, boy," Pete said, echoed by Joey. "Can we go too, Uncle Aaron?"

"We're all going," Aaron said. "Felicity is going to ride Quiche. Don't worry, honey," he reassured her. "I won't let anything happen to you, and Quiche has never jumped a fence in her life. We're going to start with the basics, so you'll know everything that's going to happen. By the time your mom comes to town, you'll be riding like a pro."

Felicity cast him a doubtful look. "If you say so. Have you got another pony about the size of Donatello?"

"You can ride Donatello, Felicity," Pete offered eagerly. "But he won't rear up like Rhyolite did." It was clear Pete found this a failing on Donatello's part.

"Once was enough," Felicity said firmly. "I'm interested in a horse that knows only one thing, and that's how to walk straight ahead at a nice, slow pace."

"Michelangelo can trot, Felicity," Joey urged. "You can ride him."

"We're giving her too many choices, boys," Aaron said, grinning. "She'd better concentrate on riding Quiche for right now. She can ride the ponies in a few days, after she's mastered the basics."

Felicity rolled her eyes. "That might take longer than you think."

"We've got time," Aaron said, holding her gaze with his own. "We've got all the time you need, honey. We'll go slow and easy, until you feel comfortable."

"My, you cowboys sure know how to make a woman feel safe." Felicity gave him a smoldering glance from beneath her lashes that made him long to remove the flashy turquoise blouse she wore so he could make love to her again. "In fact, why don't we just declare me an expert rider and let's all go have some of Polly's iced tea?" she added.

Both little boys protested this and offered the use of their ponies if only Felicity would accompany them on the ride.

Felicity sighed and put on an expression of long-suffering. "My, you cowboys sure know how to get your own ways, don't you?"

"We excel in that." Aaron thought the satisfaction he felt in just looking at her went all the way to his bones. "Cowboys want what's best for everybody concerned, and something tells me that what's best for a cowgirl is knowing how to ride a horse."

Chapter 12

Felicity reflected on that remark often over the next week. She had to admit, Aaron knew what he was talking about. He proved to be a patient, thorough riding instructor, and before she knew it, she found herself riding Quiche with increasing confidence around Aaron's property.

To her further gratification, people driving on nearby roads often slowed or came to complete halts in order to thoroughly absorb her riding garb. Of course, anything she wore was not your everyday riding gear, so she took to carrying her card case in her pocket when she rode, just in case. Business was business.

She hired people to clear out her grandmother's old furniture and trash and repaint and fix the locks, then rented furniture and moved back in, carefully stowing her most valuable items at Aaron's. Since she spent her days with him, and he spent his nights with her, the arrangement worked well. Aaron even took her to a car wash and showed her how to clean the love bugs off her truck. It required lots of special cleaners and even more elbow grease, but she finally got them off, only to begin reacquiring a new batch on her clean truck grill.

Still, Felicity thought she had never been happier in her life. Aaron made her feel cherished and sexy—so sexy he couldn't resist her.

Her cell phone rang on the day of Becky's arrival. She reached across Aaron to grab it and flip it open.

"Hello, Mama," she yawned. "What are you doing up so early?"

"I'm on the way to see my baby," Becky said. "Ain't that reason enough for a mother?"

"What time will you arrive?" Felicity squinted across the room at her little alarm clock. "I'll come meet your bus."

"High noon, baby," Becky said. "That's if we don't run into no traffic jams or accidents. My show ain't until five o'clock, so we'll have plenty of time to visit." She added hopefully, "How's things with Aaron coming along?"

Becky retained high hopes, despite Felicity's determination not to allow a hint of her affair with Aaron to reach her mother. Becky believed Felicity spent her nights at Aaron's home after the break-in, and Felicity encouraged that belief without actually saying anything.

"Fine, Mama. He's looking forward to your show. Everyone is." Felicity yawned again. "We went to the festival last night and rode some of the rides, and your show was all everyone was talking about."

"He took you to the festival?" Becky repeated. "Are we talking 'date' here, or are you going to try and say it was a family outing again?"

"It was a date," Aaron said, nuzzling Felicity's neck. "All our dates are family outings."

Becky shrieked. "What's he doin' in your bedroom at this hour, Felicity Clayton? And don't try and tell me you ain't sleeping with him, because I'm calling you a liar right here and now."

"Now, Mama—" She poked her elbow into Aaron's side as he snuggled against her.

"We're sleeping together," Aaron said.

Becky let out a loud huff of air. "Well, shut my mouth, and thank you, Jesus." She added, "I was getting worried about you, baby. It ain't natural for a girl your age to avoid men the way you always did. Not that I can say I blame you, considerin', but there are nice men like Aaron out there, and it's high time you found yourself one."

On that note, Becky hung up, adjuring her daughter to appear at the festival site the minute her bus arrived.

"She told me she was worried that her career had given you such bad experiences with men, you might never give someone genuine the time of day," Aaron explained. "So she's doing whatever she can to further my cause. You know me. I'd never turn down help from your mother."

Felicity subsided when he pulled her beneath him and proceeded to further his own cause. She had to admit Becky sounded thoroughly pleased with the news. But it remained to be seen what would ultimately come of her affair with Aaron. After all, they had known each other for barely two weeks. It was way too soon to speak of a future together, even if she was secretly looking around at empty shop spaces in Foxe.

By the time she had accompanied Aaron to his home, Felicity found herself still undecided about going home to Nashville. Her shop needed her presence, and ordinarily she would have wasted no time hurrying back to it, but Aaron had derailed her thoroughly from her career path...it was all his fault.

She loved him. It was that simple.

That meant she was up the proverbial creek without a paddle, and at any moment, her canoe might begin taking on water, if all he wanted was an affair.

• • •

"Now, folks, I've got a special surprise for you," Becky Lozano yelled into the microphone.

She wore a denim Cosmic Cowgirl outfit that showed off her slim figure on the outdoor stage in the Festival Park. The small bleachers and the wide grassy area around the stage were filled to overflowing. People had turned out by the hundreds for the performance. Becky's powerful voice hardly needed a microphone, but the crowd's enthusiasm threatened to drown out her words.

Felicity shifted and searched the crowd for Aaron. He had already left for the evening when Felicity drove up to his front door to pick up his sister and nephews. Some problem at work was keeping him, she decided. All the local businesspeople had booths and displays at the Rice Festival, and much of Aaron's time the past week had been devoted to planning his display.

"I've got a special song comin' up, especially in honor of my baby and her daddy," Becky said. "Folks, these are really, really special songs to me because they've been lost for over twenty years. So you're the first audience to hear them since I sang them to my husband way back before my baby was born."

Felicity decided the time had come to discretely vanish. In another few minutes, word might spread that Felicity was the "baby" of the songs. She gave Joey's little hand into Deborah's keeping and said something about going to find Aaron.

It took her almost ten minutes to make her way through the crowd. Becky launched into a song with a haunting melody and an opening verse that began, "Look at what loving you has given me." As much as Felicity would have liked to stay and listen, she knew she might wind up in tears. She made it a habit to always listen to Becky's new songs for the first time alone in her bedroom.

The grounds were largely deserted now that Becky Lozano's performance was underway. Felicity found Aaron at last, dickering with an old farmer over the proper cost of a new double-cab pickup truck. He looked up and smiled when he spotted her slim red jeans and lace-trimmed white western blouse. She had deliberately toned down her outfit, but she liked knowing that to Aaron, she was as eye-catching as ever.

"Hi, honey," Aaron said. "Are you hiding out from your mom's show?"

"She's singing her old songs for the first time," Felicity said, with a grimace. "I'd like to avoid going to jail for disorderly conduct tonight, so I cleared out. The first person who says anything to me about the consequences of Mama's love, or anything else…" She trailed off with a growl that made him laugh.

"I'll remember that," he said, still chuckling. "You might as well go look at the exhibits. I'm going to be tied up here for a while longer."

If there was one thing she understood, it was the business of selling. She gave the old farmer her prettiest closed-mouth smile and obligingly walked toward the exhibit pavilion, where quilts, canned goods, and many other home crafts were on display.

Scanning the crowds around the stage, she caught sight of Joey being carried away by a man she didn't recognize. Worse, that same man held Pete's hand and was clearly sneaking them both away from the crowd. She looked around frantically. Deborah probably hadn't yet noticed the boys' absence. Felicity followed the man, wondering what she should do. She shoved people aside, apologizing as she went, and raced up the booth-lined street toward the parking area. Someone was kidnapping Pete and Joey in broad daylight. She had to stop him.

The crowd was so thick that she couldn't make much headway. Felicity fought her way forward, watching helplessly as the distance between her and the children lengthened. She thought about yelling for help and decided against it. Something about the suit-clad kidnapper told her there was more to this scenario, and that she'd be wise to check into it first.

The man led the children to a silver SUV that was double parked in the road and helped them in. Felicity called out the boys' names, but before she could reach them, the car doors slammed shut and the SUV headed off down the narrow, crowded road toward the highway.

She ran across the field that doubled as a parking lot in search of her truck. Thanks to traffic in and out of the Festival grounds, the SUV couldn't get much of a head start on her. While she drove, she dug out her cell phone and called Aaron. Naturally, his phone was off while he spoke with potential customers. Next she tried Deborah, even though she knew Deborah kept her phone in her bedroom, turned off lest her husband phone her. Finally she called Aaron's home, but even Polly had deserted the house for festival activities.

She almost passed the silver SUV when it unexpectedly turned in at a motel and restaurant just outside the town. She parked beside the SUV and leaped out, wondering what to do or say next, while the kidnapper calmly stepped out of his vehicle and opened the door to help Joey out.

Felicity was outraged. "Just where do you think you're taking these children?"

The man turned and assessed her calmly. He was a handsome, dark-headed man, dressed in a suit and tie, and not much taller than she was.

"Who are you?" he asked. Even his voice was pleasant and non-threatening.

"That's Felicity, Daddy," Pete said. "We told you about her. She chased off the mean old ghost that was trying to get us. Daddy is taking us to the beach, Felicity. Can you come with us?"

Felicity stared, even though she had suspected as much. So much for the idea that Tony had been a football player. "*You're* Tony Sachitano?"

"I am." He looked sharply at her. "I suppose you've been listening to Deb."

Everything inside her went limp with something akin to relief—or laughter. "It's nice to meet you at last. Why are you sneaking off with your sons?"

"Why did my wife sneak off with them two months ago?" Tony shrugged and smiled at his two boys. "She still hasn't told me what made her run home to her big brother. So I thought I'd see to it that she has to talk to me."

Felicity tried to look severe. Tony Sachitano didn't look like a man who'd terrorize a woman. The trustful way Pete and Joey leaned against him backed up that observation.

"You couldn't just knock on Aaron's door?" she asked.

"Deb would probably flee out the back door." A charming, ironical smile played across his mouth. "She won't even talk to me on the phone. In fact, I seem to have scared her so badly, she needs a little help in facing me."

Felicity admitted to herself that she found Tony Sachitano an extremely attractive, non-threatening man, but how could she possibly know what he was like as a husband? And if he really had been seeing another woman, he deserved trouble from his wife.

"Are you telling me you're kidnapping your own children to give Deborah a reason to face you?" she asked carefully.

"I'm now a desperate man." Tony laid a gentle hand on each boy's shoulder. "My wife refuses to talk to me about what went wrong between us, so I'm forced to take desperate measures."

Felicity comprehended suddenly. "I see. You're going to let her track you down so she can face you in the heat of anger and demand her children back."

"That's right. I've left a message with Polly to make sure she won't have any trouble finding me. You aren't thinking about interfering, are you?" Tony's face took on a steely, determined look. "Because, if so—"

"Who, me?" Felicity shook her head, realizing she was looking at a man desperate to get his family back. "I think I'll just have a cup of coffee before heading on back to the festival."

"In that case," Tony said, "please join us for a snack. Afterward, the boys and I are spending the night here. Deb should have no trouble finding us."

Felicity gathered Tony had already rented a motel room and had the entire situation well-planned. She just hoped Deborah followed the script Tony had written and faced her husband once and for all.

And she hoped Aaron had enough sense to invent a good reason why he couldn't accompany Deborah on her trip to rescue her children.

• • •

Aaron stole a glance at his watch and scanned the fairway. Becky Lozano's performance had ended and the area around the food booths filled up with people once more. Aaron exchanged greetings with various friends and acquaintances and searched the crowds for Felicity.

"Aaron," Deborah shrieked over a small throng of people between them on the fairway. "The boys are gone. They've vanished—I can't find them anywhere."

"Calm down, Deb." He waited until she reached his side and put a comforting arm around her shoulders. "There's no need to get hysterical. They probably went off to look at the exhibits with Felicity."

"But I can't find Felicity anywhere, either," Deborah said, trembling. "And no one has seen them."

Aaron studied the passing crowds from the vantage point of his greater height. "They might be visiting Ms. Lozano's travel bus. The boys would find that interesting, I'm sure."

He wondered why Felicity had taken the boys without telling anyone. Surely she knew how anxious Deborah became when she lost sight of her children.

"Let's go check Ms. Lozano's bus," he said soothingly. "The musicians are probably loading their gear, so someone will be able to tell us if Felicity and the boys are there."

He knew he shouldn't leave his display, what with potential customers on the move again, but he was heartily fed up with babysitting five new Chevrolet trucks, not to mention that leaving Deborah unsupported went against all his instincts.

"Can't you call her cell phone?" Deborah asked hopefully. "She usually has it in her pocket."

Aaron reached for the phone attached to his belt. "Sure, honey."

He had turned his phone off while talking to prospective customers. He switched it back on and noted the message indicating several missed calls, including one from Felicity. He highlighted it to call, and she answered immediately.

"Are the boys with you?" he asked, watching Deborah scan the crowds anxiously. "Where are you?"

"I'm at the Foxe Highway Motel, in the restaurant," she said. "Why don't you send Deborah over to join me?"

"The Foxe Highway Motel?" Aaron understood immediately and turned away, even though Deborah was questioning passersby. "I gather Tony has come for his family at last."

"That's right. You cowboys are always so quick on the uptake," she added sassily.

"All right. I'll see to it that Deb appears." He glanced in the direction of the stage, where an enormous clot of people moved slowly in his direction. "Your mother's show is over, in case you're interested."

"Good. I'll be leaving here shortly, just as soon as Deborah arrives, in fact. Mama still has to sign about a million autographs, and do a few interviews, so she won't be done there for another couple of hours, at least."

"I've got news for you." Aaron peered down the fairway. "It may be even longer than that. The stage is still swamped."

"In that case, I'll just linger over my coffee. As soon as Deb arrives, I'll leave."

"See you soon, honey."

But the minute Aaron clicked off his phone, he noted that the people-swamped stage area roiled in a peculiar way, with a column of people following behind one charging figure that plowed through the crowd like a bullet. He watched a moment, curious, then turned aside to answer Deborah's anxious question.

"Felicity is at the Foxe Highway Motel with the boys," he said as calmly as possible. "She says you might want to join her there."

"The Foxe Highway Motel," Deborah exclaimed. "Why on earth—? Tony."

"It wouldn't surprise me in the least," Aaron said. "Tony is probably taking a few steps of his own to find out why you left him. You'd better get on over there and talk to him."

"How dare Felicity help him kidnap my boys?" Deborah clenched her fists, trembling. "I would never have thought it of her."

"I don't think she did any such thing," Aaron soothed. He watched the stream of people flowing toward him with interest. "Most likely, she saw what was happening and followed him."

"Then why didn't she make him give them back?" Deborah demanded with a sob.

"I think you're going to have to be the one to do that," he said.

Aaron narrowed his eyes and saw Becky Lozano forcing her way frantically through the crowd.

"Aaron," she yelled, when she spotted him. "That weasel has kidnapped my baby. I need to borrow your truck."

Aaron wondered why Becky would call Tony Sachitano a weasel when she didn't even know him. "Sure, Becky. I'll come with you, and you can tell me what's going on."

"Aaron, you can't leave me alone to face Tony." Deborah clutched his arm. "I just can't face him by myself."

"You're going to have to, Deb." He regretted leaving Deborah to find her way to Tony on her own, but Felicity was right. This was one battle he would be wrong to help Deborah fight. "Besides, this is between you and Tony, and frankly, you owe him an explanation."

"Aaron," Deborah wailed and clung to his arm.

He hardened his heart and turned to Becky. "What happened? How do you know Felicity has been kidnapped?"

"My band leader went to the bus and found a ransom note." Becky clutched his other arm and waved the note at him. "It says to meet the kidnapper in back of the Foxe Highway Motel and he'll tell me what he wants. It's that belly-crawling slime, Gary Carlisle. I know it is."

Aaron took the note and studied it a moment. "You think this is from Gary Carlisle?"

"I'd know that yellow-striped skunk's writing anywhere," Becky said, breathing fire. "And he'd better be there when I get there, or there'll be hell to pay."

"All right," Aaron said. "I'd better drive you. Deb, if you want to get your children back, you'd better plan on either taking your own car or coming with us. It looks as if we're all going to the same place."

"I'll skin him alive," Becky raged. "I'll make him wish he'd never heard of me or my baby. And if he's so much as laid a hand on her, I'll—"

"Better let me do it for you," Aaron advised. "You'll need to get Felicity to safety while I deal with Carlisle."

Becky turned to face the phalanx of people who had followed her. "Folks, I have to go see about my baby. Hopefully, I'll be back a little later on this evening to finish signing autographs and visiting with my fans. And thanks for coming out to see my show." She whirled and grabbed Aaron's arm.

He started toward his truck, hurrying both women along. Becky raged about what she was going to do to Carlisle when she saw him, while Deborah gasped and held on to his arm for dear life.

Beneath Becky's fury, he detected her fear and anguish. Remembering the tale Deborah had told him about Felicity's kidnapping as a child, he could understand. He wasn't feeling overly sanguine himself, although common sense told him that if Felicity was with Tony, she wasn't with Gary Carlisle. Still, who knew what the man might do, especially considering the mess he had made of Felicity's home not too many days ago.

When he reached his truck, he boosted both women up and told them to buckle in. Then he leaped behind the wheel and sped out of the parking lot as fast as possible, considering the crowded conditions on the narrow road.

Sprinting into the restaurant at the Foxe Highway Motel, he saw Felicity sitting at a table with Tony Sachitano and the boys. Gary Carlisle was nowhere in sight. Strangely, that did not comfort him. He scanned the grounds, wondering when the fellow would turn up.

Watching Becky shove open the passenger door, he considered alerting the sheriff, just in case.

• • •

Felicity looked up and spotted Aaron's truck. For a moment she felt a twinge of annoyance that he hadn't let Deborah come alone—until she remembered that Deborah and the two boys had ridden with her. Then she saw Becky Lozano, in full stage makeup and Cosmic Cowgirl outfit, come charging toward the restaurant door.

"Uh-oh," she said, astonished. "It's my mother. What—?"

Becky thrust the glass door open and plowed inside. "All right, Felicity Clayton. Where is that yellow-bellied coward? And don't try and tell me to lay off him, because this time I'm gonna skin him alive."

For a moment, Felicity thought she meant Aaron, until she saw Deborah hurrying in the door. Outside, Aaron got slowly out of his truck, scanning the area carefully as he did so.

"What on earth do you mean, Mama? Are you talking about Gary Carlisle? I haven't seen him. What are you doing here? You're supposed to be signing autographs at the festival."

"That nasty piece of slime sent me a ransom letter," Becky raged. "If he thinks he's going to get away with this—"

"That's Becky Lozano, the country singer," Tony Sachitano said, astonished. "She's your mother? And what do you know... here comes Deb."

"I should have realized she didn't have a car," Felicity said apologetically to Tony. "I drove her and the boys to the festival, so she had to get a ride. But since Mama and Aaron are here, maybe I'd better just move to another table so you can talk to Deborah in private."

Deborah arrived at the table. Her hands were balled into fists. "How dare you take my babies, Tony Sachitano? I'll call the sheriff. I'll—"

"Calm down, Deb." Tony remained where he was and smiled up at her. "I have as much right to take our sons on an outing as you have. In fact, if you're planning on divorcing me, you may as well know up front that I intend to sue for joint custody."

Deborah gasped and almost reeled with shock. "You—You—"

"Not to mention weekly visitation rights and the entire three months of summer." He dropped a hand onto each of his sons' shoulders in a casually possessive gesture.

"How dare you?" Deborah gasped.

The little boys looked from their mother to their father in astonishment. Felicity figured they'd probably never heard their parents argue before. Even Deborah looked a little surprised, as though she hadn't realized she had it in her.

"Oh, I don't know," Tony said coolly. "I guess the fact you disappeared without a word brought out the daredevil in me. I've thought of all sorts of things to dare."

Deborah went still. "You know why I left. You threatened me. Then I saw you with your girlfriend."

Tony came up out of his seat in automatic denial. "I threatened you? What the hell do you mean? I've never threatened you in my life. As for a girlfriend—"

Felicity leaped to her feet in turn. "Mama, let's you and I get that table on the other side of the room," Felicity said. "Mr. and Mrs. Sachitano need some privacy."

"He ain't Gary Carlisle." Becky glared at Tony. "How come he's leaving ransom notes in my bus and pretendin' to be that nasty old Gary Carlisle?"

"It wasn't Mr. Sachitano—," Felicity began.

At that moment, Gary Carlisle, leaner than Felicity recalled him, and with a fugitive air she definitely hadn't seen before, stepped out from the hallway that led to the restrooms.

"It was me," Gary said. "I'm desperate. Please, Ms. Lozano, I'm begging you. Rescind the charges. Let me have my life back—I'll do anything you want."

"You rat snake, you," Becky focused on him with a vengeance. "I'm gonna skin you myself. How dare you threaten to kidnap my baby?"

Felicity was thankful they were the only people in the little restaurant, although the waitress and cook both watched the scene from the kitchen.

Aaron pushed open the glass door, his entire attention focused on Gary. Such was the expression on his face, Felicity found herself stepping between the two men as quickly as possible.

"Gary, this is not a good time," she said. "Mama is supposed to be signing autographs and talking to reporters at the festival."

"There isn't a good time if this is the scum who trashed your house," Aaron said. "Get out of the way, honey. I'll take care of this."

"And I'll help you," Becky snarled, in her mother-tigress mode.

"Both of you cease and desist." Felicity felt inspiration strike in an incandescent burst of light. "There's something you need to know, Mama." She paused for dramatic emphasis. "If it hadn't been for Gary, I might never have found your songs. It's all because of him that you're singing those songs right now."

"What?" Becky almost screamed. "*He* found my songs?"

"He turned over the bookcase so that I could find them." Felicity stepped forward and took Aaron's arm in hopes of holding him in place. "They were taped to the bottom. So, actually, you owe him, Mama. I might not have thought to check there." She prayed that Aaron would say nothing.

Becky looked as if she had been struck by lightning. "*He* found my songs? Are you kiddin' me, Felicity Clayton?"

"Yes, Mama, he did." She willed Aaron not to contradict her. "So how about rewarding him by dropping those charges? You've punished him enough. He needs to get on with his life so we can get on with ours."

Aaron remained blessedly silent, although she could feel the muscles of his arm knotted into steel beneath her fingertips.

"I can't believe this." Becky looked at the ceiling and waved her hand at Felicity. "What do you think, Johnny? How can I let him get away with hurtin' our baby like that? Look at her. She's still wearin' all that metal in her poor little mouth."

Gary Carlisle tossed an uneasy glance at the ceiling and sidled back a little.

Even Felicity, long used to her mother's habit of communing with her dead father in times of severe stress, couldn't help herself. She, too, shot a quick look at the ceiling.

Becky relaxed suddenly. "Alright. Johnny says to let him go. I'll drop the charges tonight, just as soon as I get a chance to call my lawyer." She exhaled heavily, looked up once more and shook her head. "But I still think he needs to suffer a little more for hurtin' our baby like that."

"Suffer!" Gary burst out. He glared, first at the ceiling, then at Becky. "I've done nothing but suffer. I can't get a job, and my band is busted up because of this. I can't even go back home as long as those charges are pending."

Becky glared back at him. "Just you be thankful her daddy is so kindhearted, you chicken snake, you. Otherwise, I'd put you in prison to rot." She glanced again at the ceiling. "It's okay, Johnny. I said I'd drop the charges, and I will."

"Who's she talking to?" Tony Sachitano asked, eying the ceiling.

"Is it a ghost?" Joey asked, and edged closer to his father.

"She's talking to my dad," Felicity turned to give Joey a comforting smile.

"You said your daddy was dead. It *is* a ghost," Pete exclaimed. "Maybe he's the one following us."

"Not my dad," Felicity answered. "He stays with my mother."

This was a new thought to the boys. They exchanged portentous stares, then focused once more on the ceiling.

"Look, you," Becky said to Gary. "I'll call my lawyer tonight and have him drop the charges. But you'd better not ever come near my baby again. Do you hear me?"

"He won't," Aaron said, and wrapped his arm around Felicity. "If he does, I'll be the one to kill him."

"Sorry, Gary," Felicity said, grinning. "If I were you, I'd switch to rock music and play all the clubs in San Francisco or someplace like that."

Gary frowned. "Rock music? All I've ever done is country." He added plaintively, "I *hate* rock."

"Okay, then. How about blues music? You can go down to New Orleans—"

"Baby, he ain't no blues musician. I got hold of some tapes of his stuff." Becky sniffed and turned her back to Gary. "He might make it with a gospel group, but he really oughtta stay away from anything secular. If he keeps his mind on church, maybe he'll stay straight and I won't have to refile those charges."

"Gospel?" Incredibly, Gary brightened. "How'd you know I used to sing for my church all the time? Do you really think I could make it on the gospel scene?"

Becky looked over her shoulder with a priceless expression of disbelief on her face. "How the heck would I know? But if you get on out of here and go find out, maybe I won't change my mind about those charges."

"Go on, Gary," Felicity urged. "Go while you still can. Next time you try and jump start your career, maybe you'd better run it by your pastor first. Situations where someone can get hurt are nearly always bad ideas."

"But I didn't mean to hurt you," he protested. "It was all an accident. You weren't supposed to be hurt at all."

"Oh, yeah?" It was too much. Becky whirled and stalked toward him. "Well, let me tell you—"

Aaron intervened by taking Gary's arm in his powerful grip. "It's okay, Becky. I'll just escort Mr. Gospel Singer of the Year outside and make sure he's on his way out of here. If he knows what's good for him, he won't be back."

Gary looked at Becky in all earnestness. "If those charges get dropped, I won't need to come back." He twisted in Aaron's grip. "Who are you?"

"I'm Felicity's fiancé, and I'm just as unhappy about her poor little mouth as her mom is." He forcefully turned him toward the door. "In fact, if you're not out of here in the next five seconds, I'll get even more unhappy."

Becky squealed and flung her arms around Felicity. "Oh, baby, I'm so happy for you. Aaron's just the man I would have picked for you. If I thought you'd listen to me, that is."

"What?" Felicity put her hands on her hips. "I'm not Aaron's fiancé. Calm down, Mama. When I go to get married, believe me, you'll be the first to know."

"We'll talk about that in a few minutes," Aaron said to Felicity, grinning. "In the meanwhile, don't get any of your stubborn ideas, honey." He started toward the door, pushing Gary along before him.

"What stubborn ideas?" Felicity said to his backside as he went out the door. "Or is a woman's consent no longer required?"

"Law." Becky looked to the ceiling. "You better do something quick, Johnny."

"Well, well." Tony looked from Aaron to Felicity, interested. "I never thought I'd see the day when old Aaron proposed...and in public."

"You're not seeing it now," Felicity said, annoyed. "Come on, Mama. You've got to get back to the festival. Your fans are waiting for you."

"I'm not leaving this place until I see for myself that Aaron has sent that worthless Gary Carlisle on his way back to that little town in Louisiana he came from," Becky said. "Before anything else, I'm a mother. My baby's wellbeing is my first concern."

Felicity managed not to roll her eyes. "Yes, Mama. Let's go sit down over here so Mr. and Mrs. Sachitano can talk in private."

Tony said, grinning, "It looks to me as if it's all in the family, so to speak. Let's wait until Aaron gets back so my wife won't lose her courage. Sit down, Felicity. You, too, Deb."

"I'm not going to lose my courage," Deborah said in a small voice, not looking at him.

After making sure Gary was well on his way, Aaron came toward them, his gaze fixed on Felicity. She looked back at him in a challenging way. If Aaron thought he could get away with shirking a formal proposal, she had an education in store for him.

"Let's move over here, honey," Aaron said to her. "I want to talk to you."

"Better let her stay," Tony said with grim humor. "And you'd better join us, too, Aaron. Deb might crawl under a table if her support system disappears."

"I don't need a support system," Deborah said, staring at the table. "I can deal with you anytime, anyplace."

"Sure, you can," Tony returned. "That's why you spent six weeks refusing to so much as talk to me on the telephone. I guess it's a good thing I wasn't able to come before now. You might have asked Aaron to duke it out with me before I got too close."

"I don't need Aaron to fight my battles for me," Deborah stated. "You don't scare me."

"Is that right?" Tony regarded her a moment. "In that case, why don't you stop standing there and sit down with us?"

"I most certainly will." Deborah pulled out a chair and sat down beside Pete. "You aren't getting away with this, Tony Sachitano."

"I sincerely hope not," Tony said.

"In that case, we'll all join you." Aaron pulled out a chair for Becky and seated her beside Felicity. "It looks like a good day to get a lot of things settled, once and for all."

"Law," Becky said reverentially. "I sure hope so."

Pete and Joey had focused their entire attention on Becky. Every time she cast her gaze to the ceiling in silent communion with her dead husband, the two little boys' eyes followed. Felicity decided that if she didn't do something fast, the major problem in the Sachitano household would remain unsolved.

"First things first," she said. "Go ahead, Deborah. Tell Tony how he threatened you. In the meantime, the boys can come sit over here with me and my mother."

"If it's all the same to you, they'd better stay right here." Tony studied Felicity a moment then returned his attention to his wife. "Speak up, Deb. Tell me how I threatened you."

Deborah blushed and stared at the table top. "Well, that's the way I took it. You were yelling…"

"Since when does yelling constitute a threat?" Tony demanded. "The only thing I recall yelling about is your crazy idea of redecorating a perfectly good living room."

"That's the way I took it." Deborah flushed again, but she remained in place in spite of her obvious desire to flee. "You were waving your arms around and—and yelling, and—and…I got scared, that's all. Then I went grocery shopping and passed by Carlito's. You were there; with someone."

"With someone?" Tony stared at her, clearly at a loss. "What—?"

"She was very pretty." Deborah stared at the tabletop.

Tony looked stunned. "But I haven't been—" He stopped and his brows drew together. "Unless you're talking about the day I had lunch with the IRS auditor."

"You didn't tell me about any lunch with an IRS auditor." Deborah glared at him.

"I probably didn't," Tony said in dry tones. "I knew it would upset you. But I know I told you the business was being audited. The auditor was a woman, and I took her to lunch one day to continue discussing some deductions they were questioning."

"But—" Deborah clearly didn't believe this.

"Everything's fine now." Tony made a gesture of finality. "The IRS is satisfied and all questions are resolved. Are you trying to tell me you walked out on me because you thought I was seeing the IRS auditor on the side?"

"I didn't know she was an IRS auditor," Deborah said defensively. "All I know is that she was pretty, and after you'd yelled at me, what else could I think but that you were bored with me?"

"I'll never get bored with you," Tony said. "You're my wife, the mother of my children. And if you thought I was yelling at you, you should have yelled back."

"True," Felicity said, when it became clear Deborah didn't know what to say. "Just because a person yells doesn't mean he's going to hit you or leave you. Look at Aaron. He sounds like a raging lion at times, but he's actually a male cardinal. There's nothing sweeter than a male cardinal."

Aaron grinned and said nothing. The two little boys ignored their parents and watched Becky in fascinated silence.

"You should know by now that I'd never hurt you, Deb. I'm not your father." Tony concentrated on his wife. "Did it occur to you to wonder *why* I might have been upset enough to yell at you?"

"No…" Deborah began to look ashamed.

"I was worried about the business," Tony said. "The IRS was auditing us and business had slowed down. For a while there, things looked bad, and here you come wanting to throw money away redecorating a perfectly good living room."

"Why didn't you tell me?" Deborah said. "Don't you think I'm capable of understanding?"

Tony frowned. "I didn't want to worry you. Besides, we pulled through and the audit is over. Everything's fine now. With the business, that is."

Deborah sat staring at her husband in silence.

"That's no way to conduct a marriage," Felicity pointed out. "Tony, you're going to have to talk to Deborah about what's going on in your business. How's she supposed to know you're just letting off steam if she doesn't know there's anything wrong?" She smiled kindly at Deborah. "And you're going to have to give Tony time to apologize before you go running home to Aaron. It's only fair. You never gave him a chance to apologize or to explain things." She added, "You should give him at least one day to apologize before you pack up and leave."

Deborah gulped and nodded weakly.

Tony stared at Felicity. "Are you a marriage counselor or something?"

"Actually, I'm just the resident ghost-buster." Felicity rose from her chair. "I'd better leave you to discuss matters on your own, or my mother will never get back to finish signing all those autographs."

"But…" Deborah's weak protest faded. She stared at Tony.

Tony stared back. "You've got to come back home, Deb. It's like she says." He indicated Felicity. "You never even gave me a chance to apologize or explain."

"Where do you think you're going?" Aaron stood with Felicity. "Surely you aren't going to abandon the field before you're sure everything is thoroughly settled."

"I think everything is progressing satisfactorily." Felicity glanced pointedly behind him, where Tony kissed his wife like a starving man, and she kissed him back. "Now if I can just get Mama out of here before she convinces those two little boys that a ghost really is hanging around, all will be well in the Sachitano household."

"I ain't leavin' this place until I'm sure my baby is all spoken for and everything is all settled." Becky remained stubbornly in her chair. "I can't concentrate on my music if I'm all worried that some lowdown wannabe singer is romancin' my little girl and getting' her all broken up and bruised."

Felicity rolled her eyes. "Come on, Mama. It's your job to act in Daddy's place. You're supposed to be vetting any and all suitors and making sure they can take good care of me." She ignored Aaron, who slipped his arm around her waist.

"Law," Becky said. "Don't you think I already looked into all that?" She cast her gaze to the ceiling once more. "He's okay, baby. Even your daddy says so."

"You heard your mother." Aaron drew her close in spite of her attempts to hold him off. "I've passed both your parents' rigorous requirements. Therefore, you have to marry me."

"I do not." Felicity gave him a light shove. "I haven't even been asked—"

"Take that, ghost," Joey cried.

Unseen by anyone, he had produced and unscrewed the lid off a bottle of garlic powder. With a sudden jerk of his hand, garlic powder flew in a fragrant cloud toward the ceiling and showered down over Felicity and Aaron.

"Law." Becky leapt to her feet. "What on earth is that?"

"Oh, no," Deborah groaned. "Not the ghost again."

"I smell garlic," Tony said in astonishment. "Put that fork down, Pete. There's garlic powder everywhere."

In the pandemonium erupting around them, Aaron stepped close to Felicity. "Then let me remedy that right now. Miss Clayton, you are the only woman in the world for me. Will you please marry me?"

Felicity dithered. Now that the moment had come, she found herself desiring to postpone it a minute or two longer.

"My shop is in Nashville—" she began.

"Becky says you have a great manager in Nashville," Aaron said. "So what's stopping you from opening a branch of The Cosmic Cowgirl right here in genuine Texas cattle country?"

She pretended to think, which was difficult with Aaron's arms around her. "That's a good point. It would make great advertising copy, wouldn't it?"

"Especially if you combine your advertising with mine," Aaron said, equally thoughtful. "Those fancy cowgirl clothes of yours and a new Chevrolet truck...what could be better?"

"Oh, darn," Felicity said. "I knew those Chevy trucks would be a deal breaker. This is all about my truck, isn't it? You are so determined I drive a Chevy that you're willing to marry me—what a disappointment."

"Aaron, do something," Deborah screeched.

Felicity and Aaron glanced toward the table they had just left. Both Pete and Joey stood on their chairs, glaring at the ceiling, table forks in hand.

"If we had some flour, we could throw it on the ghost," Pete called. "Can you get us some flour, Felicity?"

"What is all this ghost business about, boys?" Tony rose calmly and removed the fork from Joey's hand. "Sit back down before you get us thrown out of here."

"Flour won't work on ghosts," Felicity said absently. "And with all the garlic in here, ghosts shouldn't be a problem anyway."

Becky winked at Felicity. "That's for sure. It's even run Johnny off, and I sure would have thought he'd stick around to see his little girl get herself engaged."

"I'm not engaged yet," Felicity said. "We're still in the negotiating stage."

"Why, you little heifer." Aaron pulled her flush against his body. "We've agreed on the shop and the advertising scheme. For you to stick to driving a Chevy truck instead of a Dodge...I really ought to turn you over my knee on that one."

"You just watch yourself, Aaron Whitaker, or I'll sic Joleibenshen's Benkenstein Venerschnitzel on you."

"Who?" Aaron looked around, but everyone else was busy banishing lingering ghosts.

"The prize-winning schnauzer I'm about to adopt," Felicity informed him. "His job will be to protect me from importunate Chevy truck salesmen."

"So I'll have to resort to carrying dog treats around with me all the time." He lowered his face to hers. "But I don't mind that. For you, no sacrifice is too great." He smiled. "I'll even give you one of my cows."

"Now that's the way a man ought to talk," Becky said. "Good for you, Aaron. Hurry up and say yes, baby. I've got fans waiting."

"Now, Mama, Aaron doesn't want me to say yes because you made me."

"Actually," Aaron said, "I wouldn't mind if you said yes because your mother made you. So long as you say yes."

Felicity thought about this for a moment. "All right, then. Yes. I'll marry you; but only because my mama made me."

Becky folded her arms and sniffed. "Like I ever succeeded in makin' her do anything."

Aaron lifted Felicity and turned her in a slow circle, and she happily threw her arms around his neck.

"It's all right, Mama. Aaron is going to fix me up with a branch of The Cosmic Cowgirl to run and a brand new Chevy truck to drive—that turquoise one, I think—and he's going to give me a cow of my own that I can name Elsie. Like any other good businesswoman, I'm a sucker for a great bribe."

"I'll even throw in a horse," Aaron said, grinning. "Every good cowgirl needs a horse of her own."

"In that case, you've got yourself a deal, Mr. Whitaker."

No one could say she didn't know a good deal when she saw one, and a man like Aaron Whitaker was definitely a good deal.

She had the best deal of all, Felicity realized, as he sealed their bargain with a thorough kiss. She had him and she had his love, and that was everything.

More from This Author
(From *Georgie's Heart* by Kathryn Brocato)

Georgeanne Hartfield stayed at her desk and kept on working. She had hoped skipping lunch with her coworkers would buy her some peace, but she feared she was about to be proven wrong. Worse, her stomach grumbled and complained because she hadn't expected to miss her lunch today, so she hadn't brought along a sandwich.

She bent over her work as she heard the back door to the Gant Medical Clinic open. If she was lucky, they had discovered some new topic to discuss.

"Listen to this." Nurse Denise Devereaux appeared and laid the hardback book she held down flat on Georgeanne's desk with the air of one about to reveal a secret of the universe.

Georgeanne grimaced at the sight of the book her friend held so reverently. "I have work to do, Denise. I'm not getting paid to hear Fritzi Field's sexual advice."

"You aren't getting paid to miss your lunch, either," Denise returned. "Now pay attention, Georgie."

"That's telling her, Denise." Redheaded Angela Porter joined Denise in leaning over the counter in front of Georgeanne. "The rest of us would love being paid for listening to hints on improving our sex lives."

"Quiet, y'all." Sandra Whitney, a tiny blonde pixie in her starched nurse's uniform, joined the group and leaned over Denise's shoulder to study the book. "I want to hear this. Simply everyone is talking about that book."

Georgeanne gave up. She smiled upon the other three women and propped her chin on one long, shapely hand. "Go ahead,

Denise. I can see I won't be able to get a thing done until you're through."

Georgeanne prayed Dr. Gant or Dr. Baghri would come in, even though she knew they were out for a long lunch. Whip-cracking doctors never came around when the clinic receptionist needed them to maintain order among the staff. The Gant Medical Clinic, which was located in the rural southeast Texas community of Fannett, usually stayed too busy for such frivolities as book readings.

Denise, the chief nurse at the Gant Clinic, drew in a deep, dramatic breath. She was a beautiful African-American woman with skin the color of milk chocolate and a figure fit for a Playboy magazine centerfold. "'If your husband makes your life miserable and blames you because you can't have an orgasm on demand, he has no right to complain if you resort to a little acting every now and then.'"

"She's got a point." Sandra leaned further over Denise's shoulder, her pale blonde hair brushing Denise's black pageboy, and peered at the book.

"Why all this uproar over a book on how to fake an orgasm?" Angela, the clinic's lab technician, wanted to know. "I don't have that sort of trouble."

Her tone implied *Why would anyone have a problem, unless she's a psych case?* Georgeanne looked thoughtfully at the tall, slender redhead.

"Neither do I," Sandra interjected, flushing. "But that doesn't mean I don't agree with Fritzi Field. Some women probably do have trouble. I mean—"

"Then they should read *The Sensuous Woman*," Angela interrupted. "Instead of wasting time learning how to fake it, they could be learning how to experience the real thing. Why all this uproar over something that's completely natural?"

Georgeanne never ceased to be amused at the rapid defensiveness of modern women when the subject of orgasm came up. Either every woman she knew experienced orgasm instantly, or every woman she knew lied. According to her friends at the Gant Clinic, sexual desire and orgasm behaved like an electrical switch. When you flipped the switch, lights turned on. Period.

"Childbirth is perfectly natural, too," Georgeanne said, "and look at all the books out on it."

"*Faking It* isn't about having an orgasm," Angela argued. "It's about faking an orgasm. There's a difference."

"Fritzi isn't talking about normal men," Denise said. "She's talking about complete jerks. I should know. I was married to one. Listen to this. 'Why let your marriage be destroyed, when it's so easy to give him what he wants?'

"'Many a man thinks a woman ought not to need foreplay. He thinks she ought to be ready the minute he touches her, as if the very thought of sex with him is all that's needed. Any suggestion that this may not be the way it works sends this man into a frustrated shouting and blaming fit.

"'Who needs that?'"

The women looked at each other a moment in silent agreement when Denise finished reading that passage aloud.

"Who, indeed?" Georgeanne didn't look up from her current task of comparing a column of hand-written numbers to a copy of the column in a printed report, but she knew her cheeks glowed with telltale red her thick fall of shoulder-length brown hair might not entirely hide.

One would think that a twenty-eight-year-old woman who had been married to a man who resembled a young Robert Redford would have stopped blushing when she lost her innocence. But that wasn't the way things went with her face, Georgeanne thought with resentment. If anything, she blushed even more these days. Fritzi Field's incredible and unexpected popularity, both nationwide and inside the Gant Clinic, kept her cheeks flaming. Maybe she should claim a sunburn. Or a medical condition.

"That's what I say," Sandra declared. "A man like that deserves whatever he gets."

Angela snickered and flipped her red hair off her shoulders. "Are you kidding? He's getting a heck of a lot more than he deserves. Anyone following Fritzi Field's instructions will have the idiot thinking he's God's gift to womankind." She stretched out long, white polyester-clad legs and leaned back on Georgeanne's desk. "Fritzi Field is going around telling women to award those stupid men some sort of bad-behavior prize if you ask me. She ought to be ashamed of herself."

Georgeanne bit her full lower lip. A strange, empty feeling attacked her heart, almost as if she had stepped off a porch and found no step where one should have been.

How ridiculous. Not even she agreed with everything Fritzi Field said, so why should she feel upset when someone else didn't either?

"That isn't what Fritzi is saying—," Denise began.

Georgeanne heard with horror the respectful tone in which Denise said "Fritzi" and rushed into speech. "Fritzi Field isn't trying to say anything. She's interested in creating a controversy, because controversies sell books." She added, in a barely audible voice, "I wouldn't be surprised if Fritzi Field turns out to be a man."

"Boy, is she—or he—selling books," Denise agreed. "They're trying to line her up for all the talk shows, but her agent says she wants to remain anonymous. If I had written *Faking It*, I'd go on every single talk show that would have me."

Guilt, liberally mixed with fear, attacked Georgeanne like a battering ram to the solar plexus. She paled and stared down at the report in her hand.

Angela grinned. "Oprah Winfrey, here we come."

Denise picked through the book and opened it at another marked spot. "You're just jealous because you didn't think of writing *Faking It* first. I know I am."

Georgeanne suppressed a gasp.

"Yeah," Angela said. "You're right about that much." She folded her hands behind her frizzy red hair and gazed at the ceiling. "Do you know what I'd do if I had all that beautiful royalty money pouring into my scrawny little bank account? I'd buy myself a green Mustang convertible. That's what I'd do."

"With that red hair and pale skin of yours?" Georgeanne looked up and focused on Angela's milky, freckled skin. "You know what Dr. Gant said to you about getting in the sun ever again in your young life."

Angela ignored this comment. "I'd lose five pounds, and I'd buy a tiny black bikini with those high-cut legs, then I'd go cruising down the beach highway with the top down."

"Four walls and a roof," Georgeanne said. "That's the kind of sunscreen Dr. Gant told you to use."

"If you ever made that much money, you'd gain five pounds celebrating at the nearest bar, Angie," Denise countered. "Do you know what I'd do? I'd buy myself a lot and build a beach cabin in the ritzy section of the beach. Then I'd lose five pounds and put on my red bikini with the high-cut legs and get a tan out on my own deck."

"Yeah, Denise," Angela said, laughing. "Now that you mention it, you are looking a little pale."

"I was making a point." Denise glanced at her own dark-coffee arm with dignity. "With that kind of money, why cruise the beach in a hot car? Buy yourself a big piece of the beach."

"Not me," Sandra said in dreamy tones. "I'd buy Bobby a new car to drive to work in. His old truck is about to quit, and when it does, he'll have to use my car until we can afford a new truck." She straightened and pushed her wispy blonde hair back beneath her nurse's cap. "What about you, Georgie? What would you do if you had big royalty checks rolling in?"

Georgeanne, cheeks flaming, looked up from her documents. She let her brown gaze drift back to the sheets of paper on her desk in a suggestive way. "You already know what I'd do with it. I'd make a big donation to Dr. Baghri's Saturday Clinic. We need more medicines—"

"Puh-leeze," Angela said. "You're such a sucker, Georgie. When Dr. Baghri talks about the poor little children, you just fall all to pieces and start volunteering. When do you have time for yourself? When do you date?"

"I don't," Georgeanne said, without rancor. She never wanted to date again. After her ex-husband had proved she wasn't woman enough to hold a man, Georgeanne figured she was better off avoiding trouble. "I'm too busy with the clinic."

"Well, the Saturday Clinic is a wonderful idea," Denise said. "But you can mark my words, it's going to fail. Charity clinics always fail because doctors hate to work for them."

"Not the way Dr. Baghri has it set up," Georgeanne said. "If he gets just forty doctors lined up, each doctor would only need to work one Saturday a year in the Clinic."

A brooding silence reigned.

Georgeanne glanced at her friends and couldn't resist a grin when she took in their serious faces. "What is it with you all? Are you trying to tell me I'm getting to be a bore on the subject of Dr. Baghri's Saturday Children's Clinic?"

The other three women chuckled and said in unison, "Who? Us?"

"Be reasonable, Georgie," Denise said. "I'll agree that Dr. Baghri's idea is brilliant. If every doctor around here who wants to do a little charity work would donate one Saturday a year, the Saturday Clinic would be a model for the rest of the United States. The problem is getting the doctors to sign up so the Clinic can get off the ground. Right now, it's only Dr. Baghri and Dr. Gant who are carrying the load. And you."

Georgeanne had been thrilled several months before when one of the doctors she worked for had come up with a plan to help children whose parents had too much money and pride to go to the free county clinics, but not enough money to afford regular medical care. Using the Gant Clinic's facilities, Dr. Baghri had created the Saturday Children's Clinic where office visits cost only twenty dollars per visit on Saturdays.

Dr. Baghri's plan involved having each doctor in the surrounding area donate one Saturday per year of his time. The twenty-dollar charges helped offset the expenses of keeping the clinic open, and the medications were mostly free samples donated by drug companies. Community response threatened to overwhelm the clinic, thanks to local layoffs and a generally poor economy, but doctor-response so far had been less than enthusiastic.

"I'm working on that," Georgeanne said, "and so is Dr. Baghri. We'll get more doctors signed up soon. The problem is, no one quite understands how Dr. Baghri's plan works. As soon as I get my sales pitch worked out, things will be different. And I'm thinking about a web site—"

"It isn't your fault, Georgie." Denise folded her arms, book still in hand, and studied Georgeanne in a knowing way. "If that clinic fails, don't you go convincing yourself it failed because you didn't talk it up good enough."

"That's for sure." Angela pushed off Georgeanne's desk and brushed down her clinging white trousers. "You've worked as hard for the Saturday Clinic as Dr. Baghri has. Harder."

"It won't fail," Georgeanne said. "Not after Dr. Scott's widow just donated her husband's old clinic building to the cause. Which reminds me." She turned a stern gaze on her co-workers. "This weekend Dr. Baghri and I are going to be cleaning out the building and doing some painting. We're going to need a little slave labor."

Good-natured groans arose, but Georgeanne smiled with satisfaction. No matter how much her co-workers might gripe about the encroachment of the Saturday Clinic upon their free time, each and every one of them would be present for the great paint-in Georgeanne planned.

"Do you know what I wish?" Angela gave Georgeanne an affectionate grin. "I wish that just once when we talk about winning the lottery or getting big royalty checks, you'd say you're going to lose five pounds and buy a yellow bikini and a yellow convertible."

Georgeanne laughed at that. "Come on, dreamers. Five pounds won't make a dent in this body, and you know it. As for bikinis, I think I'd feel more comfortable in one of those boy-leg swimsuits."

Good-natured hooting arose. Georgeanne smiled on her friends and shook her head when they proclaimed her figure perfect as it was. A woman who stood six feet tall and who was built on a grandiose scale to boot didn't go around kidding herself about yellow bikinis. She bought a black boy-leg suit and she draped a dark towel around her overly curvaceous body.

Still, she liked knowing her friends appreciated her as she was. She certainly wasn't likely to change, not when her every effort in that direction had met with total and complete failure.

"Honey, you aren't meant to be a skinny bean pole," Denise said. "You were born with curves, and you're going to die with curves. Unless you do something stupid."

"Like get the curves liposuctioned off?" Georgeanne asked in the meek tones of one seeking information.

Denise frowned at her. "Like develop anorexia or get that weight-loss surgery. You wouldn't look right if you starved yourself down to nothing."

"Oh, give us a break." Angela walked over to gaze idly out the tall window facing Georgeanne's desk. "You're beautiful as you are, Georgie. And if you weren't so busy being soft-hearted, you'd take pity on some of the men who keep falling all over themselves trying to get you to notice them."

"What men?" Georgeanne asked. "If you're talking about poor Mr. Spector, who tripped over his little boy yesterday—"

"Brent Spector is just one of them," Denise said. "You don't see all these single fathers gazing at you when you aren't looking, but we do."

Since the Gant Clinic specialized in pediatrics, any man old enough to be gazing at Georgeanne was a father. As for men falling all over themselves to gain her notice, Georgeanne found that ridiculous.

"Let me demonstrate the way they look at you." Denise leaned forward with a sheeplike expression so full of wide-eyed longing, Georgeanne almost burst into laughter. "They're all dying to stroke those curves of yours, honey. Men think you look like a real woman."

"That's probably because I look like the motherly type. Single fathers don't need wives. They need mothers for their children." Georgeanne gathered up her papers once more.

"You don't see yourself, Georgie," Sandra said. "Men love the way you look."

Georgeanne reflected that if she had a nickel for every time she'd heard that statement or one like it, she'd be able to buy herself that yellow convertible.

"If I listened to my loyal friends, I'd be impossible to live with." She stood, papers in hand. "I'd better get these into the mail right away, or Dr. Baghri will have no one present when he dedicates the new Saturday Clinic building."

Angela pulled aside the translucent curtain and peered out the window. "Dr. Gant and Dr. Baghri just drove up. Who's that with them? Oh, my God. I'm having a heart attack." She grabbed at her chest. "Serious hottie alert, ladies." She fanned her face. "Now there's a man a woman could have an orgasm just looking at."

"Where?" Denise rushed over to join Angela at the window. "Oh, wow. He looks like a movie star. Say, I think he is a movie star. I know I've seen that face before. Isn't he the guy who played Tanner Colt in *Deuces High*?"

Sandra joined the group. "It is him. It's Hunter Howell."

"I expect it's Dr. Zane Bryant," Georgeanne said. "I've been writing him on Dr. Baghri's behalf." She went to the counter separating her cubicle from the waiting room and began folding letters and slipping them into envelopes. "Haven't you heard the story? Hunter Howell and Dr. Bryant are identical twin brothers. They were separated at birth and adopted out to different families. They found each other several years ago when Dr. Bryant saw Hunter Howell in a movie and contacted him."

"I don't care if he is just a doctor," Angela declared. "If he's coming in here, I'm going to get his autograph. He's seriously, seriously hot."

"He's coming in here." Georgeanne went back to her desk and rustled through her top drawer for stamps. "He practices pediatrics in Pasadena, and he's very interested in Dr. Baghri's idea. He wants to learn firsthand how the Saturday Clinic operates."

Pasadena was a suburb of Houston within easy driving range of Fannett. Georgeanne smiled with satisfaction, recalling the regular letters and emails she had written on Dr. Baghri's behalf to Dr. Zane Bryant over the past few weeks. She had been as thrilled as Dr. Baghri when Zane Bryant asked for an appointment to view the new clinic. The request meant her skills in coaxing reluctant doctors into donating time to charity showed improvement.

"Oh, please," Angela groaned. "Don't tell me all he's going to be talking about is charity clinics. What a waste."

"You don't mean that," Georgeanne said with gentle reproof. "You were the first person to volunteer when Dr. Baghri couldn't get a lab tech for the Saturday Clinic."

"Well, tell the world, why don't you?" Angela stared out the window. "If a woman was married to a man who looked like that, she wouldn't need Fritzi Field's advice on how to fake it."

Georgeanne's face flamed, and she wished for the millionth time that she wouldn't blush every time anyone mentioned Fritzi Field. One of her friends might draw the correct conclusion any day now: Georgeanne Hartfield had a guilty conscience.

Two years ago, Georgeanne's handsome husband left her for another woman. During the period immediately after her divorce, Georgeanne had produced a book. The writing had assuaged her anguish and helped her come to terms with her dead marriage.

The book had blessed her in more ways than one. It had been excellent psychological therapy, and the money from its sale helped finance Dr. Baghri's clinic and bought dog food for the Humane Society, among other things.

Georgeanne simply hadn't expected the book to take off the way it had, much less that it would be waved in her face every day at work.

Lord help her if anyone ever realized Georgeanne Hartfield was the reclusive, controversial author, Fritzi Field. Everyone would know she had lost her husband because she was lacking as a woman, and Georgeanne didn't think she could stand that.

The group at the window scattered. Angela hustled back to her lab and the two nurses scurried off in opposite directions.

Georgeanne remained at her post, pasting stamps on the envelopes she had already addressed. She would get a close-up view of Dr. Zane Bryant soon enough. Besides, a woman who had been married to a man who resembled Robert Redford knew better than to let a man's good looks sway her common sense.

The front door opened and three men entered. One assumed an instant prone position on the floor when a blue toy car flew from beneath his foot and bounced off the wall.

"Dr. Bryant!" Aghast, Georgeanne rushed through the swinging door that separated her from the waiting area and knelt beside him while Dr. Gant and Dr. Baghri gazed down in paralyzed horror. "Are you all right? Oh, this is all my fault. I didn't see that car when I straightened the office this morning. I'm so very sorry."

"It's not your fault, Georgie," Dr. Gant, a tall, thin man with graying hair said in stunned tones. "Cleaning the office isn't your job in the first place."

Georgeanne winced. That meant the clinic's regular cleaning woman, who was at home nursing her sick mother at Georgeanne's insistence, might be in trouble. If only she could learn to think before she spoke.

"My apologies, doctor." Vijay Baghri, a short Indian man, joined Georgeanne in kneeling beside Zane Bryant's prone figure, and his small dark hands joined Georgeanne's efforts in assisting Dr. Bryant. "Dr. Gant will perhaps hire a new cleaning person."

"Not on my account, please," Dr. Bryant said. "The truth is, I was born clumsy."

Georgeanne gave a sigh of relief. There lay a rare man indeed, a young good-looking doctor who wasn't so stuck on himself, he sought revenge on anyone who placed him in a ridiculous position.

"It was my fault," she said in firm, no-nonsense tones. "That truck wasn't there this morning when we opened, or I'd have been the one on the floor. Here, Dr. Bryant. Let me—"

Then Georgeanne met the fallen doctor's gaze and found herself as breathless as if she had taken the fall herself.

Laid out full-length on Dr. Gant's blue carpet, his black hair disarranged by the fall and tumbled across his forehead, Dr. Bryant lay perfectly still and stared up at her. The way his smoky, gray eyes focused on her in such a dazed fashion, she feared a concussion.

Oh, he was a stunningly handsome man all right, but handsome men were as litigious as ugly men, especially when an incident involved damage to their self-image.

He kept staring at her, and Georgeanne felt the full focus of his attention with an unprecedented, purely feminine sensation she found almost as disturbing as her fears of concussion.

She took herself in hand. Dr. Bryant had come to learn about Dr. Baghri's Saturday Clinic. Her job was to promote the clinic with every fiber of her being. Nothing else mattered.

•••

Zane Bryant rolled over and looked up from his nose-down position on the floor. He found himself face-to-face with a goddess. Or an angel. He wondered if more than the breath had been knocked out of him by the unexpected fall.

She was almost as tall as he was, and she had soft, candid, dark-brown eyes framed with incredibly long, curling lashes that reminded him of a doe's eyes. She had skin like that of a porcelain doll, all pink and white, and full red lips that needed no lipstick.

Moreover, she was soft with lush feminine curves, and the hands that supported his shoulders were long and strong and slender, the hands of a woman who wasn't afraid of work. She looked like a woman who valued people more than she valued intangibles. Or a career, he added in his mind.

In spite of many self-lectures about the folly of imagining virtues into a woman just because of the letters and emails she wrote, Zane knew he was guilty of exactly that.

He didn't really know her yet, he reminded himself. That's why he was here.

Zane came to himself at last and realized he still lay on the floor like an idiot. He let them assist him to a sitting position and tried to gather his wits.

"Miss Hartfield?" he wheezed. Damn, but he'd taken quite a fall. He wished he wasn't so clumsy. Talk about making a miserable first impression on a beautiful woman.

She smiled and looked relieved. "Yes, I'm Georgeanne Hartfield. This isn't the way we wanted to welcome you, Doctor."

"I can assure you, I'll never forget my first sight of you." Zane smiled and placed one hand over his heart while he remained seated on the floor. She smelled of lilies. Zane decided lilies were his favorite flowers. "Keep your cleaning woman, Dr. Gant. She just did me a great favor."

Georgeanne laughed. Zane considered the warm glow of gratitude in those gorgeous brown eyes an unexpected reward.

"The doctor does not need our help to get himself to his feet," Dr. Baghri said in his humorous, broken English. "Our Georgie will lift him up by his heart."

Georgeanne blushed. "Hush, Doctor. You'll have our guest thinking I do heart transplants on the side."

Zane Bryant stared again in spite of his fear that Georgeanne might consider him rude. This magnificent creature actually blushed. If she was the Georgeanne Hartfield who had been corresponding with him on Vijay Baghri's behalf for the past few weeks, his good fortune looked too incredible to be true.

He rolled to his feet and reached down to help Georgeanne up. She stood only a few inches shorter than he did.

Splendid, he thought.

He wasn't aware that he still held her hand and gazed at her face until Dr. James Gant cleared his throat in a meaningful way.

"Thank you, Dr. Bryant." Georgeanne withdrew her hand with a startled look. "I'd better get back to work. Dr. Baghri's letters are almost ready to go out. We're dedicating the new clinic location in a couple of weeks."

"I hope I'm invited," Zane said.

Georgeanne gave him a swift, impersonal smile. "Of course you're invited. If you'll stop by my desk on your way out, I'll see to it that you get your invitation this afternoon."

Zane wondered if he could get out of touring the Saturday Clinic so he could get to know Georgeanne. Or better, if he could talk Georgeanne into acting as his tour-guide.

Georgeanne directed another smile in his direction and hurried back to her desk where the telephone sounded an insistent appeal.

While Zane pretended to listen to Dr. Baghri's discourse, he noted that Georgeanne apparently reached the phone too late, because it stopped ringing. She looked at it in a regretful way and reached for some papers on her desk.

A dignified black woman in a white nurse's uniform appeared at the counter behind Georgeanne's desk. Georgeanne looked up with a warm smile. Zane wished she would direct all her smiles at him.

"Who was on the phone?" he heard Georgeanne ask.

"Mrs. Miguez is holding for Dr. Baghri," the black woman said. "Tammy's asthma is acting up again, and she's panicking."

"Oh, dear." Georgeanne looked distressed and stood at once. "Dr. Baghri says she may have to be hospitalized this time. I'd better put him on immediately."

"Have you seen my copy of *Faking It?*" the nurse asked. "I thought—there it is. You put your papers on top of it."

Georgeanne glanced at the book on her desk and turned scarlet. Zane searched his memory but couldn't immediately place the title. He resolved to look into the matter further. Anything that caused this incredible woman to blush interested him.

"What is it with you?" the nurse asked. "Every time I so much as mention this book, you do an imitation of a boiled lobster."

"We have a visitor," Georgeanne said, almost choking. "Would you mind getting that silly book off my desk?"

"What for?" the nurse asked, grinning. "Are you afraid the visiting doctor might see it and make a few assumptions?"

Georgeanne ignored that and hurried out of her office cubicle. She approached the doctors and spoke a few sentences in Dr. Baghri's ear.

Zane watched her approach, smiled at her, and wished she would come close enough to speak in his ear. To his intense interest, she returned his smile and hurried back to her desk.

The telephone rang, and Georgeanne answered it without looking up when Zane crossed the room and glanced around her small cubicle.

"Yes, Mrs. St. George," she said. "Yes, that's the one. Thank you for telling me."

Zane watched the smile that crept over her face with deep interest. She laughed, and Zane found himself equally fascinated by her full, rich chuckle.

"The article is based on my observations from working in a children's clinic for several years," she went on. "I'm so glad you enjoyed it." She listened a moment. "Well, someday I hope to have children of my own, of course. One of these days, when Mr. Right comes along."

Zane's mind filled in the other side of the conversation. Georgeanne had written an article. That didn't surprise him at all, considering the way he'd been pouncing on her epistles for the past few weeks.

What did surprise him was the image that rose in his mind of Georgeanne with a dark-headed baby at her breast. In his years as a pediatrician, he had seen many, many women with babies at their breasts, but none of those real images rocked him the way the vision of Georgeanne did.

All he had to do to make it come true was convince Georgeanne she had at last met Mr. Right.

For other titles by this author, check out
Old Christmas, and *Sutherland's Pride*

In the mood for more Crimson Romance?
Check out *Lake Effect*
by Johannah Bryson
at *CrimsonRomance.com*.